MURDER AT CROWSETT

Basil C. Hampshire

MINERVA PRESS
MONTREUX LONDON WASHINGTON

MURDER AT CROWSETT
Copyright © Basil C. Hampshire 1996

All Rights Reserved

ISBN 1 86106 227 3

First Published 1996 by
MINERVA PRESS
195 Knightsbridge
London SW7 1RE

Printed in Great Britain by
B.W.D. Ltd., Northolt, Middlesex

MURDER AT CROWSETT

In memory of my wife Kathleen, a lovely, gentle lady.

All characters in this book are fictional, and any resemblance to any person, living or dead, is purely coincidental.

MURDER AT CROWSETT

Monday, March 27th

Dorothy Shervell, the illegitimate daughter of the Widow Shervell, was twenty-two years old when, on the night of Sunday, March 26th, she was murdered in a local wood known as Rabbit Shaw in the village of Crowsett which is in the County of Midshire, but her body was not discovered until 6.45 a.m. the following morning.

Also of significance on that night was a sudden, extreme drop in temperature, exceptional for late March, which reached its nadir in the early hours of Monday morning.

Tom Farrar, known in the village as Young Tom to distinguish him from his father who was also named Tom, a farm labourer employed by Henry French, came across the body while taking a short cut through the Shaw, a move he would not have contemplated normally, given its evil reputation, had he not been late for work in French's high meadows. Tom was eighteen years old, a sturdy lad with an open face and tightly curled fair hair. He was of medium height, and his large hands and feet he had inherited from his mother. Engaged to Lucy Sweet, he hoped to be married the following year.

He regretted his decision as soon as he crossed the plank bridge over the mill stream and entered the forbidding interior of the Shaw. Only half-light filtered through the close-packed trees, and the intense cold had coaxed a shin-high, white mist from the previously warm earth. Nevertheless, he pressed ahead, following a track rather than a path, and soon found himself halfway through the wood in a fairly large clearing. It was then, looking to his right, that he saw the body lying on the ground facing away from him. It was obvious from the high-heeled, brown ankle boots she wore, and the white, woolly pom-pom hat, that it was a female. The only female known to him, from local gossip, who used the Shaw regularly was Dorothy Shervell, known variously as Dottie, or the Goat Girl, or by some as a Witch.

Witch or not, she must have fallen and hurt herself or collapsed from the cold, and Tom moved slowly forward to make sure.

Close to her he could see that blue jeans were tucked into the boots and that she also wore a darker blue anorak. Placing a tentative hand on her left shoulder, he gave it a little shake, and the body rolled slowly towards him on to its back, revealing the still recognisable face of Dottie. But the face was a mask of horror, the eyes wide open and staring (at him it seemed), and the lips drawn back to show tightly clenched teeth in a rictus of death.

To add to the horror, her arms were held partly out, stiff, as if in supplication.

The hands were clawed, and a patina of frost covered the body from head to foot.

Looking more closely he could see spots of blood on the white jumper she wore under the anorak. He almost retched when he saw that tightly embedded in her neck was a length of thin rope or wire, a necklace of death.

Hot bile rose in his throat, and moving quickly to behind the nearest large tree, he vomited up most of his recently eaten breakfast. Pausing for one last look at the body, Tom took to his heels and bolted out of the Shaw, over the plank bridge, and along Mill Lane to the cottage where he lived with his parents and younger brother David.

Ethel Farrar was forty-nine years old, and for most of those years she had been working either in the fields and orchards owned by Henry French or the hopfields owned by Bertram Ovenden. Her seamed, brown skin, and callused hands bore tribute to this, but her hair was still fair with only a few grey streaks. She was a big woman in every way, but not fat.

She was sitting in front of a glowing kitchener drinking her third cup of tea and leafing through a women's magazine lent to her by May Upton, her neighbour and friend. Gas was laid on, but Ethel had cooked and warmed herself with and by the kitchener since her marriage twenty-seven years ago.

Tom, her husband, had left for work with his friend Jack Upton shortly before Young Tom, who had mislaid one of his boots. Upton was foreman at the mill and oast owned by the Ovendens, and Tom was his deputy.

A placid woman, and not easily startled, Ethel was nevertheless taken aback when the kitchen door burst open and her son was framed in the doorway, his face had a greenish pallor and his mouth was working but he was unable to speak. Taking him by the hand she led him to the chair next to her own and sat him down.

"Something's happened, I can see that. Was it Broadbridge because you were late?" (Broadbridge was French's foreman and something of a tyrant.)

"Take your time, son."

Her calm manner and soothing words did the trick.

"Oh Mum, it was awful, in the Shaw..."

"What were you doing in the Shaw?"

"I was late, wasn't I, and I wanted to make up time, so I took a short cut, and I found her..."

"Found who?"

"Dottie Shervell, she's been murdered." He put his hand to his mouth.

"Mum, I've been sick and I've got to go again," and he bolted to the outside lavatory.

"Murder!" Mrs Farrar said to herself. "Murder in our village! Why, it's absurd."

"And Dottie Shervell? Surely he didn't meet her in the Shaw? Oh no!" Tom returned and sat down again.

"What have you been up to, Tom? Are you telling me the truth?"

"Yes, that is the truth. I was walking through the Shaw and I came into this clearing and there she was, lying down. I thought she was hurt and went over to see. I touched her shoulder and she rolled over. Mum, it was horrible. Her eyes were open like she was staring at me, her teeth were clenched like, her arms stuck out, and she was covered with frost. Then there was this rope or wire round her neck, tight, so I knew she had been murdered. It was awful." He put his hands over his face.

"You didn't have anything to do with it, did you Son?"

"Of course not, Mum. She must have been laying there for hours – she was as stiff as a board.

"Can I please lie down, Mum? I do feel bad."

"Alright Tom. Go in the front room and strip down to your pants. There's a fire in there because it's so cold. I'll bring you a blanket."

Having seen him tucked up, Mrs Farrar threw a shawl over her head and shoulders to protect her against the cold, and said:

"I'm going next door, Tom, to use the phone and tell Mr Bennett. Stay there and if Davey comes down, don't frighten him; tell him I'll be back to get his breakfast"

Tapping on the Upton's kitchen door, Mrs Farrar said, "It's me May, Ethel, I'm coming in."

"Eth, whatever is it, you look like a ghost?"

May Upton was the exact opposite of Ethel Farrar. Thin and tall, and as the wife of the foreman for Ovenden she enjoyed newfangled things, and everything she had in the kitchen was the latest and the best.

"It's Young Tom. I'm all of a skimble-skamble, May, on account of what he told me about when he took a short cut through the Shaw..."

"He was daring, wasn't he?"

"He was late for work. Anyway, he came across Dorothy Shervell lying on the ground and when he went to see if she was hurt, she'd been murdered."

"Never, not in Crowsett. Was he sure?"

"Yes. He told me exactly how she looked. Horrible, he said. She'd been strangled and must have been lying there for hours.

"Can I use the phone to speak to Mr Bennett?"

"Strangled! Yes, of course you can, Eth."

Frank Bennett was a police sergeant attached to the Kimpton force, Kimpton being the nearest town to have a fully-manned force.

He was forty-three years old, had served in the Royal Navy for twelve years, in the Metropolitan Police for ten, and had returned to Up Markham, where he was born, five years ago, when he made sergeant. Officially he was the community policeman for five villages: Down Markham, Up Markham, Crowsett, Magpie Revel and Shackleford. He was married with two daughters, both married and both living abroad. He was allowed a police cottage and a police car equipped with telephone. His wife was named Joan. Broad, rather than tall, he had dark hair, a broken nose from boxing in the Navy, and the perfect manner to go with his post. He had a sense of humour, and was liked and respected (as one of them) by all those he dealt with.

"You're an early bird, Mrs Farrar. What can I do for you?"

"Mr Bennett, it's Young Tom. While he was going through the Shaw…"

"Hold on, Mrs Farrar. What was he doing in the Shaw?"

"Taking a short cut, he was late for work. He's never done it before and I wish he hadn't done it this time. He found Dottie Shervell. He says she's been murdered, strangled with a rope or something…"

"Was he involved, Mrs Farrar?"

"No, Mr Bennett, he says not and I believe him. He said she must have been there for hours, she was as stiff as a board."

"He's not pulling your leg, is he, Mrs Farrar?"

"You wouldn't ask that, Mr Bennett, if you'd seen him when he came in. He's been sick twice, and I've got him lying down in the front room wrapped in a blanket."

"Have you told anyone else, Mrs Farrar?"

"Only Mrs Upton, I'm using her phone."

"Yes, of course. Please don't tell anyone else, I wouldn't want a crowd milling about. I'm going now to speak to Mr French to ask him to spare two of his men to keep people out. Do you want me to tell him about Young Tom?"

"Please, Mr Bennett, he's in no fit state to go to work."

"I'll tell him. Thanks for letting me know, Mrs Farrar. I'll be in Crowsett as soon as I can."

"What was all that about, Frank?"

Bennett hadn't noticed that Joan was beside him.

"Hang on, love, I must speak to French."

"Henry, Frank Bennett. There's been a murder in the Shaw…"

"Pull the other one, Frank, April Fool's isn't until Saturday."

"I mean it, Henry. The girl, Shervell, she's been strangled. Young Tom Farrar found her."

"What the hell was he doing in the Shaw? He should have been up in the high meadows harrowing."

"He was late, Henry, and he was taking a short cut. You know how Broadbridge can be if hands are late…"

"With my approval, Frank."

"I know, you're a hard man too. What I want is a couple of men, if you can spare them, to guard either end of the Shaw until I can get uniformed PCs there?"

"It'll cost you." He heard French laughing.

"Don't worry, I'll see them in The Pilgrim's. Will you do it?"

"Yes, alright, Frank"

"Thanks a lot, Henry." He thought for a minute. "Henry, are you still there?"

"What now?"

"Tell them not to go inside in case they interfere with any clues; I want one at the top end, the other at the entrance over the plank bridge. I'll be there as soon as I can, and when I've had a butcher's I'll phone the Inspector at Kimpton"

"You heard, Joan, I must get to Crowsett as soon as possible."

"But you haven't had any breakfast, Frank."

"Give me a cup of tea, love, that'll do for now."

When he was fully dressed, his wife brought him the tea and said:

"Here's a piece of fried bread I was saving for your breakfast. Eat it on the way. Goodbye love."

The road was icy, and Bennett had to drive the four miles to Crowsett carefully, to avoid skidding. The fried bread was forgotten until he reached Coopers Lane in Crowsett, when he ate it after parking away from the entrances to the stables and French's farmhouse.

Fortunately, there were only a few people standing in Mill Lane opposite the Shaw, and it did not look as if anyone had gone in. He dispersed the sightseers, warning them that the lane would be needed for several cars to park in later on.

Alf Maxted, one of French's men, was standing guard at the entrance, and Bennett crossed the bridge and joined him.

"Sorry to lumber you with a job like this when it's so cold to be standing about, but I can't get anyone from Kimpton until I've been in and had a look and phoned the Inspector."

"Don't worry, Frank; we'll be looking for you in The Pilgrim's."

"I'll be there. Who's at the other end?"

"Sam, Sam Goss."

"I'll have a word with him after I've seen the body."

"Rather you than me, Frank."

"You can say that again."

In his time in the Met. Bennett had seen many horrible sights but this one capped the lot, and he was hard put to keep the little he had eaten from going to join Young Tom's mess under the tree.

Before leaving the Shaw, Bennett had a word with Sam Goss, promising him that he would see him in The Pilgrim's Rest at a later date.

Taylor was in the CID room at Kimpton police station, and Bennett was put through to him.

"Buck, it's Wiggy, there's been a murder in the Shaw; a local girl named Dottie Shervell –"

"Come off it, Wiggy. This is Monday 27th March, not Saturday, April Fool's Day. I came in early to deal with the burglary job and you start telling jokes"

"Listen, Buck, a girl has been murdered in Rabbit Shaw. She was found by a young lad named Tom Farrar. I have been into the Shaw and I have seen the body. She has been strangled. Can you believe that?"

"Keep your cool, Wiggy. You must admit, murder in that little village is a bit hard to swallow." His tone changed. "What have you done so far? Is the Shaw guarded, and what do you need immediately?"

"I got here only fifteen minutes ago but the Shaw is safe. Henry French lent me two men to guard either end; they will need to be replaced by uniformed PCs. We'll need screens for either end and the blue and white tape. I'll try for an incident room if you want to operate from here rather than Kimpton, and I've got to collect the girl's mother to identify her, plus a statement from the lad."

"Right. I'll get busy this end."

"Will you be coming?"

"I'm not sure. DCI Brotherhood's in Kimpton General having his piles seen to, hopefully with satisfaction to him and to all of us, so Bloxham may turn it over to Yarborough, to the Task Force."

"We shall need an incident room there. I'm going to alert the Quack and the lab people now, but for the moment it's up to you."

"Thanks Buck, I hope it will be you. Remind all the bods who will be coming that they will have to park in Mill Lane. If you remember there's only a plank bridge over the Mill Stream to get to the entrance to the Shaw."

*****

Bennett went first to Cowmeadow Lane, to the cottage where Dottie Shervell had lived with her mother. His path to the front door was barred by a large billy goat with an impressive spread of horns. He remembered that Henry French had allowed Alice Shervell to have a few of his herd, which had been looked after by Dottie Shervell, on account of the Widow Shervell's father having a fine herd in his lifetime from which French had drawn the nucleus of his own flock. The goat lost interest when Bennett didn't move, and wandered away, allowing him to make a quick sortie to the front door, and to use the knocker. The door was opened by Alice Shervell. She was of medium height, her face was tranquil and unlined, and her hair snow white. Her eyes were washed blue and she had the ability to look a person straight in the eye, and the mind, too, it seemed. She was wearing an old jumper over the long skirt that trailed around her feet and sandals. Among some of the villagers she had the reputation of being a witch due, most probably, to the accuracy of her fortune-telling with her tarot cards.

She looked straight at Bennett and said, "She's dead, isn't she? It was in the cards, it was always in the cards. Is she in the Shaw, Mr Bennett?"

She did not appear to Bennett to be either surprised or grief-stricken at the news when he said that she was. He said, "I would like to take you to her so that you may identify her, and I will bring you back. But you must prepare yourself for a shock."

Alice turned and went inside, reappearing wearing an old coat but no hat or gloves.

She sat in the back of the car and the journey passed in silence. Standing in front of her daughter's body she bent down for a moment and straightened up, saying, "It's her," and she turned away to go back to the car.

At her front door Bennett said, "It will be necessary for you to make a statement concerning Dorothy's movements last night and some other matters, and someone will be along to take it."

"I can tell you little," she said and went indoors.

Bennett's next call was to the cottage in Mill Lane to see Young Tom Farrar and get a statement from him. He was still lying, wrapped up, on the sofa in the front room and looked pale and shaken. He had little to add to the information given to Bennett by Mrs Farrar, but Bennett made a few notes and left to make his last call, the Rector,

Rev. Ernest Cottew, who, being a bachelor, had opted to live in one of the two bungalows in Church Lane in preference to the Old Rectory with its many rooms. He was happy to allow the police to hire the church hall until Saturday in the first instance provided that the usual terms applied, especially those relating to smoking and drinking, and to the replacement of anything broken. He would arrange for the meters to be read before and after the hiring was complete. Bennett promised that he would be provided with a claim form in due course.

Turning the corner into Mill Lane, Bennett saw that the 'circus' had arrived and congratulated himself for having the foresight to park in Coopers Lane.

A uniformed PC, he saw that it was Dick Parker, had replaced Maxted at the entrance to the Shaw which was shielded by a screen and the customary blue and white tape.

He could also see that Inspector Taylor had come and was standing on the stretch of green outside the entrance, together with his DC, David Blackwell. He crossed the bridge to join them, meeting his friend with relief. "Hello Buck, hello Blackie, am I glad to see you."

"Hello Wiggy. You nearly didn't. Bloxham wanted to turn it over to the Task Force at Yarborough but they turned it down because of staff shortages: the flu bug and men and women on courses. But he gave us until Saturday by which time things will have improved in Yarborough. Us means you as well, Wiggy, you've been seconded to me for the duration, Lampitt's your replacement pro tem, but don't worry, you'll get your patch back when this is over, or we are replaced."

"Do we get to keep the car?"

"Yes, I made it a condition."

"Have you been in yet, Buck?"

"Yes, I went in with the Quack. Not a pretty sight. Who spewed in there?"

"The lad who found her, Young Tom Farrar."

"Why 'young'?"

"Because his father is also Tom. I've got the lad's statement. He was still shocked and couldn't add much to what he told his ma. I've also got an incident room, the church hall."

"What about the mother?"

"She was really weird. When she opened the door, before I could say anything, she said that 'it was in the cards, it was always in the cards,' she meant her tarot cards that she tells fortunes with, and she asked me if she was in the Shaw. I told her I'd come to take her there.

"When she saw Dottie's body, she bent down, straightened up and said, 'It's her.' When I left her at her door and said we should need a statement later on she said, 'I can tell you little.'

"That won't do. We'll send young Blackwell to charm a statement out of her. What about it, Blackwell?"

"Anything you say, Inspector."

Looking at the three men standing together, Blackwell stood out. He was taller by an inch or so than Bennett and Taylor, good-looking, with dark hair and a pleasant smile, and an air of confidence about him. Taylor was a pale man, greying hair, lips a thin straight line, nose sharp with creases running down either side to meet similar ones either side of the mouth, but it was his eyes that caught the attention. So pale to be almost white, they had earned him the nickname 'Sharky' or 'The Shark' among the criminal fraternity in the Met.

While Bennett was in uniform, the other two wore their own 'uniform' of dark anoraks over dark trousers and black shoes. Neither wore a hat.

The doctor came out through the screen.

"Morning Sergeant, I don't know this chap."

"He's my DC, Sir, Blackwell."

"Your first murder, Blackwell?"

"Yes Sir."

"You haven't been in yet?"

"No Sir."

"I've seen many in my time, Inspector, but this one caps them all. I suppose it's the cold that makes it worse, the arms for example. Any estimate of the time of death would be a guess. Let me know later when she last had food and what she ate and it would certainly help.

"Anyway, what we have is a well-nourished female in her twenties, killed by a length of rope pulled tight round her neck with so much force as to crush her thyroid cartilage, Adam's apple to you, causing almost certain death. Your killer must have exceptionally strong wrists to accomplish this. In a way it reminds me of something in a book I read by John Masters about the Thugs in India. It might be a copy except that it wasn't a weighted scarf which was used, and the killer left his 'weapon' behind which a Thug would never have done... "

"An amateur, Sir?"

"Possibly, but whoever it was panicked, I would say.

"No sex involved, and no robbery judging by the untouched handbag lying there.

"One interesting feature: there was a laceration on the third finger of her left hand, the engagement finger, or possibly the marriage one, where it was obvious a ring had been torn off, and I mean torn off. A jealous husband, or boyfriend?

"I've already made one comment about the time of death. Rigor mortis, which goes down and then comes up again, doesn't help in this case because of the cold, but if you twisted my arm I would guess between eleven and twelve last night.

"One thing I forgot: I don't know whether she could have had a go at the killer because her hands were clawed and I couldn't get a good look at her nails. That will be for later on when we have her on the table. Let me know about the food as soon as you can. Good day to you."

"Your turn, Blackwell, see what you make of it!"

"Tell me about the girl, Wiggy."

"She won't be missed, she was bad, rotten to the core."

"Why specifically?"

"You name it, Buck, she did it. Men for money, stealing and on top of that she had the reputation of being a witch. For example, she stole a gold watch from old Porritt who's renting the Old Rectory. Swore blind she hadn't taken it and when I searched the cottage, not a sign. And she was always in the Shaw, and you remember the reputation it had.

"How old?"

"Twenty-two or twenty-three, not bad-looking, until you see her in there, it shook me..."

"I know her mother tells fortunes, what about her father?"

"Shervell's not her father, or wasn't, because he's dead. The story is that one afternoon a gypsy called at Alice's door asking for a glass of water. She took him in, and he filled his boots. He never came back and Alice was left in the club.

"Apparently Shervell couldn't get it up, and when he found Alice was pregnant he knocked her about, took all the money in the house and scarpered to The George And Dragon at Shelbourne. He bought drinks for the house saying he was going to be a pa. They believed him, and when he went to leave, drunk as a fiddler's bitch, they followed him out. He got halfway across the road and turned to wave and got knocked down and killed by a lorry. The people who saw it swore blind it was the driver's fault and Ovenden, Shervell used to work for him, was able to get Alice a settlement from the owners sufficient to keep her for life. And he gave her a small pension on top of that.

So Dottie's pa was Mr X."

"You told me about the Shaw once when we were kids. Why its reputation?"

"Years and years ago it was used by what they called satanists and witches. They used to sacrifice, animals and humans, they reckon, and you can still see part of the stone altar they used. It's got this magic sign carved into the base, a pen-something. It's in the clearing where she was found. That's a connection for you."

"So what we've got," Taylor said, "is a scrubber, a bastard, and a witch all rolled into one. A suitable pedigree to attract a killer, wouldn't you say, especially if he was a client? Any takers, Wiggy?"

"Only one comes to mind: fellow called Lee, works for Woodman at the stables. He and Dottie were close, rumour has it. Anyone else? Stick a pin in any one of her clients, including at least half the darts team."

"If Blackwell doesn't do the trick with the mother I'll eat my hat."

"You may have to, Buck. Crowsett people are a tight-lipped lot. Here's Blackie now."

"Well?"

"Not a pretty sight, Inspector, you were right. Incidentally the forensic chaps asked me who was sick in there and I told them. They were grateful. The doctor covered it all except for one thing, with which he wouldn't have been concerned. I think she knew the killer because she must have been facing him..."

"Why, to both statements?"

"I was looking at the girl's boots, high-heeled boots, and behind her right boot was a definite indentation in the ground. That would have been caused if she had been facing him and turned her back on him, felt the rope round her neck and tried to turn back but too late because her heel caught in the earth."

"Yes, it could have happened like that. That's good, Blackwell. Anything else?"

"I had a close look at the rope round her neck. It was not too thick and I think it may have been part of a lead rope used for horses. My father has a couple like it. From the weave, the little I could see of it, I'd say it was custom-made."

"The forensic people will confirm that when they get the rope off her neck.

"So, if she was facing him and turned her back on him, the killer must have drawn her attention to something behind her..."

"Or she heard something," Bennett suggested.

"That's possible too, Wiggy. We know now that the killer is not only strong, but an amateur, unless it was a pro who panicked, and cunning.

"You did a good job, Blackwell, and as a reward you are elected to pay a visit to Alice Shervell, who is a reluctant witness, and charm her into giving you a full and frank statement: who Dottie knew, what kind of others she knew besides Lee, and what she was really like. And, of course, the info the Quack wants.

"When you're through we will be in the church hall, I hope. Do you..."

"Yes Inspector. But I don't know where Mrs Shervell lives,"

The Sergeant answered, "In Cowmeadow Lane, it turns off Coopers Lane which you see behind you. Go straight down to the end and turn left into Cowmeadow. The Shervell cottage is the last one on the right-hand side."

"Thanks Wiggy."

Blackwell was on his way when Bennett called out to him, and Blackwell stopped and turned.

"Look out for the big goat, Blackie."

"The what? The big ghost?"

"The big goat."

"Oh, thanks."

"Does she have goats?" Taylor asked

"Only a few French let her have. Dottie used to look after his goats, that's why she was known as the goat girl in some quarters."

"Here's what I want you to do now, Wiggy. Take Parker, I shall be here for quite a while and I'll cover for him, and do a house-to-house. It shouldn't take you too long. The relevant time you will be asking about is between eleven and twelve, maybe a quarter to eleven to make sure.

"Get some grub on your way back, stuff for sandwiches, tea and coffee and soft drinks. No beer or liquor, I don't want anyone interviewing smelling like a brewery."

"Don't worry, Buck. The Rector warned me, and no smoking."

"What about money?"

"No problem, Buck. Hayhoe'll give us tick for the time being. I'll tell him he can claim it back."

"On your way then, Wiggy. Parker."

"Yes Inspector."

"I want you to go with Sergeant Bennett on a house-to-house. He'll fill you in.

"OK Wiggy, I see Mike coming out, so on your way."

Mike Martin was in his forties, head man on the small forensic team. He said as he joined Taylor, "Not much to go on, Buck. I'm glad your DC told us about the spew; we thought we might have to analyse it.

The ground's still as hard as iron, and the only prints we found are those of the girl coming in which must have been before the frost settled, half-past ten, quarter to eleven. How Chummy got in, short of flying, is a mystery unless he wore socks.

"We'll let your CS, Bloxham it still is, isn't it?" Taylor nodded assent, "Have our report as soon as possible."

"Can the body be moved now?"

"Yes, I'll send the ambulance crew up."

Taylor waited until the crew reappeared from the Shaw with the stretcher. The body was enclosed so far as was possible given that her arms were still frozen.

"You didn't find it easy," Taylor said as they passed.

"You could say, Inspector, that this was the stiffest stiff you could have." With this macabre witticism they moved over the bridge and on to the ambulance.

Taylor watched until she was stowed away, thinking to himself that all bad she might have been but she didn't deserve a death like she had suffered.

He went into the Shaw for a last look round and called to PC Norris who had replaced Sam Goss at the far end to come down to the front to take Parker's place.

"I'm going to have a last look round before I phone Kimpton. They will send a transit van to collect the screens and tape. You can then go to the church hall which is the incident room. You know where it is?"

"Yes, Inspector."

"There will be reporters who will try and come across the bridge. Keep them out. This is the only way they can get into the Shaw. The other way in means a walk right round the village which they'll know nothing about. If I'm not here tell them to wait."

"I will, Inspector."

Taylor went into the Shaw and into the clearing. Now that the body had been moved he could see clearly the small indentation. Blackwell had mentioned that there were no other marks visible so his theory held up. Coming out of the Shaw he saw a group of reporters, led by Ted Billings, chief reporter for the local rag, and a stringer for one or possibly more London tabloids, turning into Mill Lane from the High Street.

"I'll get rid of them," he told Norris, "and then I'll go to my car and talk to Kimpton. But follow my instructions to the letter."

"Good morning. What can I do for you?" he said, facing them.

"We understand there's been a murder. We'd like to know some details?"

"There has been a murder in Rabbit Shaw..."

"What's a Shaw?" one of them asked.

"What you see behind me, a wood. This one happens to have had a lot of rabbits in it at one time.

"A girl, a local girl named Dorothy Shervell, has been murdered. She was strangled. We are investigating, but we have no suspect at present. A further bulletin will be issued from Kimpton Police Station in due course.

"Just a word about protocol: this is a small, remote village, and the villagers are a close community who do not talk easily to strangers. I would ask you, therefore, to respect their privacy.

"Thank you for listening."

"It's a bit of a change for you, Harry, after the Met."

Taylor saw that it was one of the reporters from *The Express*. He had been one of the few friends Taylor had made among the London newsmen.

"It suits me, Alan. It means I don't have to bother with you lot too often." He smiled.

"One more thing: take pics outside the Shaw until it's placed on limits. PC Norris won't like it if you try to get in beforehand."

The reporters turned and went back, to the High Street no doubt, looking for local colour. They already had enough coverage of the outside of the Shaw. Taylor watched until he saw them turn the corner into the High Street, before going to his car to telephone the Chief Superintendent, George Bloxham. He briefed him about the position so far, mentioning the incident room which he hoped he could use to save too many journeys into Kimpton. He got permission for that and for them to take meals in the incident room. He didn't get a WPC, but he did get a tape recorder.

He asked too for a transit van to be sent to pick up the screens and tape. He told Norris to wait until the van had come for them before joining the others at the church hall. Norris knew where it was.

Taylor got back in his car and drove to Church Lane where he parked the car behind the hall.

Blackwell had found his way to the Shervell cottage and, as Bennett had warned, he was confronted by a large goat. Mrs Shervell must have been watching, for the front door opened and she called out, "Go away, Lucifer, you old fool," and the goat obediently moved away to join the others. Blackwell produced his warrant card.

"I am Detective Constable Blackwell, Mrs Shervell, and I would like to ask you some questions concerning the death of your daughter. May I come in?"

In the good-looking young man, Alice Shervell saw the ghost of another young man who had come to the door one hot summer afternoon over twenty years ago asking for a glass of water. She had asked him in and, before she knew what was happening, she had found herself in bed with the young good-looking gypsy, and for the first time in her life, she became a real woman. Her marriage was a sham, and Alice knew it could never alter. The gypsy promised to return but never did, and she was left with only a memory and an unwanted pregnancy to try and explain to her husband, who had been unable to consummate their marriage.

The memory was still there, and she welcomed Blackwell as a relief from life with a daughter she hadn't wanted, and who hadn't wanted her. They sat in the front room and Blackwell noticed the coloured cards on the table at which Mrs Shervell was seated.

"Would you like some camomile tea, Mr Blackwell?"

"No thank you, Mrs Shervell. Are those tarot cards?"

"Yes, I tell fortunes with them. I cast them for Dorothy many a time and the result was always the same: her death was bound to happen."

"Rather a strange question, Mrs Shervell, but will you tell me at what time you ate last night before Dorothy went out, and what you ate. It will help to establish at what time she was killed."

"We had supper at eight-thirty, like we always did. Last night we had bread and butter with cheese on top, toasted under the grill, and goat's milk. That was her favourite."

"What time was it when you saw her last?"

"Twenty minutes to eleven. I went up to bed at a quarter to ten and I read in bed; Dorothy was downstairs. I heard her come upstairs and go into her bedroom, but I did not notice the time. I assumed she was dressing to go out; she had said she might. When she came into my room at ten-thirty she was dressed as she was when I saw her this morning. 'I'm going to see someone special,' she said, and by the way she smiled when she said it, I knew it must be him."

"Who, Mrs Shervell?"

"Why, Lee, Joseph Lee. He works at the stables. They were engaged; he gave her a ring, she showed me it."

"Was she wearing it when she left, Mrs Shervell?"

"Yes, she was. Then I knew it would be Lee. I could also have told when she smiled like she did."

"Would you tell me everything you know about your daughter: anything which may have given someone reason to kill her?"

She sat back in her chair. She appeared to him to be looking inwards rather than at a particular object. After a while she said:

"Dorothy was bad. It was my mother's fault mostly. She came to live with me when father died, and it was the biggest mistake I ever made. After Dorothy was weaned I went back to work at Markham Manor, at Lady Markham's request: she was having difficulty getting staff. That meant that Dorothy was in the care of my mother for a long time.

"She told Dorothy stories about Jane Corby, one of our ancestors. She even called Dorothy, 'Jane'. I didn't want that. Dorothy was helped by the White Witch, Jane Corby was the Black Witch..."

Blackwell realised she must be talking about the film *The Wizard of Oz* and wondered what was coming next. Taylor would have a field day. Alice must have read his thoughts.

"You look as if you do not believe, Mr Blackwell, but Jane Corby was a real person. She was tried as a witch by the elders of this village many centuries ago, and condemned to be burnt at the stake, and she was, on the stretch of ground beyond the fence where the goats are, known at that time as the Devil's Ground. Some still call it that. When she was burning but still alive she called out that her power should pass to every second girl child born into a Corby family. She is believed to have said that because her own illegitimate girl child was smothered at birth.

"My father was Luke Corby, Dorothy was a second child after me who was the first born to my mother. Dorothy was born on the same day and date in the same month as Jane Corby, and she died on the same day and date of the same month as Jane. And she will burn like Jane. That is why Dorothy believed she was Jane Corby reincarnated, an idea my mother put into her head."

Alice put her hands over her face to hide her tears. When she spoke of Dorothy burning, obviously she meant cremated.

"Would you like to stop, Mrs Shervell?"

She put her hands down and reached into her pocket for a handkerchief.

"No, thank you. I must tell it all.

"At sixteen she was going with men for money. When Miss Lesley gave her a part-time job helping her at the Old Rectory, she stole, including the old gentleman's gold watch. They told her to go. The Sergeant came here looking for it but she had hidden it away, in the Shaw I expect. That's where she hid everything. I could not tell the Sergeant because I was afraid of her, afraid of my own daughter."

"Mrs Shervell, what you have told me about your daughter and Jane Corby, is it really true?"

"Every word. The Rector told me; I went to him for help. He has parish records going back hundreds of years. He urged me to persuade Dorothy to come and see him but, of course, she refused."

"Could I ask you now what friends she had besides Lee?"

"She kept that to herself, but I would not have called them friends. She confided in me where Lee was concerned; I think she was in love with him, and that was unusual."

"That's all then, Mrs Shervell, and thank you for being so patient at what must be a difficult time for you. All that you have told me will be most useful in our investigation."

"Perhaps we shall meet again, young man, I have a feeling we shall. I will cast the cards for you and be able to tell you something of your future. When were you born?"

"Second of July, 1968."

"The sign of the crab. You are as sensitive as your birth sign would indicate. Goodbye for now."

"Goodbye, Mrs Shervell, and thank you again."

"And don't take any notice of Lucifer. Just say 'shoo' and he'll go."

Lucifer was waiting for him, and Blackwell said 'shoo' and Lucifer went. At the junction with Coopers Lane he turned and looked back. Mrs Shervell was still at the front door. She waved and he waved back.

*****

The incident room, as the church hall was now to be known, was fully operative when Blackwell arrived. A large trestle table had been set up in the main hall. On the table was an enormous teapot, a carton of milk and two plates of different kinds of biscuits, plus spare cups and saucers. Parker and Norris were sitting at the table facing the door on stackable chairs.

He greeted the two PCs and Parker said, "Welcome to the church tea-rooms, Blackie. Want a cuppa?"

"Please Dick. Milk and one lump."

"Coming up."

"Where are the Inspector and the Sergeant?"

"In the office, at the back," Norris answered.

Parker handed him the tea, "Alright Blackie?"

"Fine, I'll take it in with me. Stand by for an explosion."

"Well, good of you to join us, Blackwell. I asked you to charm her not move in with her," Taylor greeted him.

"When I first came to Kimpton, Inspector, you told me a cardinal rule when conducting an interview. Let the person talk, listen, and wait for the little nuggets of information which, hopefully, will be forthcoming. I did just that, and I think it paid off."

Bennett did his best to conceal a laugh, and even Taylor smiled.

"Touché. That's what they say, isn't it, in the best circles. Never mind your nuggets for the moment, I want to get the results of the house-to-house on the tape recorder. I couldn't get a WPC, therefore no typewriter!"

"But Buck, there's a typewriter in the cupboard over there."

"And I can type with two fingers, quite fast," Blackwell added.

"No typing. If we can't have a WPC we'll put everything on tape and one of them at the station can type from the tapes."

He switched on the recorder and set the scene.

"One. From Mrs Woodnutt, owner of The Pilgrim's Rest. Alibi's the darts team, some of whom may have been suspects in the murder of Dorothy Shervell, because they were playing a match at Shelbourne, left Crowsett at eighteen-thirty on Sunday night and didn't return until two a.m. Monday morning.

"Reports, in confidence, seeing Joseph Lee, a suspect, in a car driven by Mrs Rose Callender, widow, living at the White House in Crowsett.

"Two. Eli Twiss, shepherd employed by Henry French the farmer, reported that his collie, Nell, barked and scratched at the door of his cottage, and finally howled, at a time he estimates to be eleven, twenty-three hundred hours, on Sunday night. Significant because Nell was a favourite with the dead girl who brought her extra milk when she had pups.

"Three. Michael Leask, Lucullus, Church Lane, said he was posting a chapter of his latest book. But he was seen by Flora Poste, owner of a wool shop and sub-post office, leaving Reeves Alley, next to her shop and the Tithe Barn, crossing the road and meeting the Rector, Rev. Ernest Cottew, at the corner of Church Lane, where they both have bungalows. The Rector did not tell the truth either.

"Both men will be interviewed and asked where they really were at twenty-three hundred hours on Sunday night."

Taylor switched off.

"Before I switch on again for your little nuggets, do you want the whole of it in one go, or would you rather pick out bits?"

"Pick out bits, some of it you won't believe. I'll give you the bits you'll want if you switch on."

Taylor did so, and pushed the microphone across to Blackwell.

"Interview with Mrs Alice Shervell at 24 Cowmeadow Lane, Crowsett, time 09.00 and 11.15, Monday, March 27th.

"Dorothy Shervell was engaged to Joseph Lee, who works at the stables in Crowsett, and is a possible suspect in the Shervell murder, and was wearing a ring which he had given her when she left home on Sunday night to go to the Shaw. This was probably the one torn off the girl's finger.

"The Shervells last ate at eight-thirty, and had bread and butter with cheese on top toasted under the grill, and goats milk. She left home at ten-forty and said she was going to see someone special. Mrs Shervell was certain it was Lee."

Taylor switched the recorder off.

"Hang on. Wiggy, get that information about the food and time over to Kimpton and ask them to get it to the Quack!" He switched on again.

"Go ahead, Blackwell."

"Mrs Shervell said a lot about an ancestor named Jane Corby who was burnt as a witch centuries ago. Apparently, Dorothy thought she was this Jane reincarnated because they shared the same birth dates, both were the same age, and both were illegitimate. Jane is said to have called out a curse, as she burned at the stake, on every second girl child born into a Corby family. Dorothy's grandmother was a Corby, so was her mother, therefore, and counting from Alice Shervell, who was Mrs Corby's only girl child, Dorothy was a second child." Taylor switched off again.

"What's all this mumbo-jumbo got to do with this case?"

"Its all true, Buck," Bennett said as he came back into the office. "Have you got any more weird nuggets, or is that it?"

"Yes, the rest is about the girl who, her mother said, was bad right from the start, including going with men for money when she was sixteen, and stealing.

"But she didn't know of anyone else who was close: Dorothy was really in love with Lee, she thought."

Taylor slapped his hand on the desk.

"This changes things. Let's go back to what Minnie Whatsis said about Lee and Rose Callender together. If Lee was Jack-the-lad with women and was carrying on with Rose, he wouldn't want to be tied to a no-future wife like Dottie, and that could be a motive for murder. Is Rosie rich?"

"She's worth a packet, Buck. Her husband sold the family business in India and with what his parents left him, she's rolling in it."

"What about this for a scenario? Lee arranges to meet her in the Shaw, having already made up his mind to end it. He takes the rope with him and probably picks a quarrel. She's facing him so he calls her attention to something behind her. She turns and he has her. Taking the ring in case it could incriminate him, he panics and leaves the rope behind. Anyone who can handle a stallion weighing a couple of tons would have the strength the killer did.

"I know that it looks to be circumstantial but it's the best I can come up with so far."

"What if we're on the wrong track altogether, Inspector?"

"Have you got something better to offer, Blackwell?"

"Not better, Inspector, but an alternative. I'm thinking, about the remark the Doctor made concerning thuggee."

"How many Indians are there in Crowsett, Wiggy?" Taylor said and laughed. "One Anglo-Indian, and three others who have experience of India. Rose Callender is part Indian, and Porritt and his daughter, who live at the Old Rectory, lived in India for years, he worked for the government and she was born there. Then there's Edmund Kehoe who lives in Cowmeadow Lane, he was thrown out of an Irish University they say and was sent to be a tea planter in India"

"Didn't you tell me he was the village drunk, Wiggy?"

"Maybe I was exaggerating a bit, but he can put it away. Fortunately he does most of his drinking indoors."

"I suppose it could have been the other way round, Rose wanting to get rid of Dottie, but it's thin. I still think Lee is number one.

"Nevertheless, we will still have to see those four, if only to make Blackwell happy, three perhaps if we exclude the girl. What's she like, Wiggy?"

"Lesley, she's a lovely girl, you can count her out."

Taylor switched the recorder on.

"So we shall be interviewing the Rector, Michael Leask, Mr Porritt, Mr Kehoe and Joseph Lee, and Mrs Rose Callender." Taylor switched off.

"Who does Lee work for?"

"Stephen Woodman, he and his wife, Buck, run the stables in Coopers Lane." Taylor switched on again. "And Stephen Woodman, Lee's employer.

"I will be explaining the reasons when I see the Chief Superintendent. Inspector Taylor off."

"When are we eating, Wiggy?"

"And what are we eating?" Blackwell added.

"I'll find out, Buck."

Bennett disappeared into the main hall to reappear with PC Parker.

"I have been elected chef for today," Parker announced, "and you can have cheese or ham sandwiches, or cheese and ham toasted sandwiches because I found a grill-thing like we have at home. With tea and coffee, of course, or a soft drink."

"Toasted sandwich and coffee for me, please Chef."

"Thank you, Inspector, and you other gentlemen?"

"The same," they echoed.

"Thank God someone still has a sense of humour.

"Interviews, I'll take Woodman first, then Lee, then Kehoe. Wiggy, I want you to take the Rector and Leask."

"I don't think I'd get much out of Leask, Buck, earlier today he was as rude as he could be."

"Scrub Leask then. Blackwell, you can have him. And because of your undoubted charm you may have Porritt (or, of course, his lovely daughter) and Rosie Callender.

"By the way, we should have someone on hand all the time, I mean CID, and I'm afraid that means you, Blackwell."

"Where does he sleep, Buck?"

"There must be a heater in the kitchen, and it's got warmer."

"I've got a better suggestion, Buck. If Up Markham isn't too far away Blackie can stay with me. How about it, Blackie?"

"Fine, if Mrs Bennett is willing."

"She will be."

"That's settled then. You'll have to put a notice on the door with your phone number on it, Wiggy, and your name, Blackwell.

"Now, we're on a tight schedule today. I have to be back in Kimpton by five at the latest. That means any interviews not completed by, say, four-fifteen, will have to be held over until tomorrow."

Parker put his head round the door.

"Ready, Inspector?"

"Yes, wheel it in."

*****

The time was close on one-thirty when they had finished eating, and Taylor and Blackwell started out, leaving Bennett the short walk to the Rector's bungalow.

Taylor left Blackwell at Reeves Alley to walk through into Coopers Lane and Woodman's Stables, leaving Blackwell to continue down the High Street to the Old Rectory which stood opposite The Pilgrim's Rest.

On his way across Coopers Lane to the stables, Taylor met a hatless youth, a gypsy-type with coarse good looks which would be attractive to a certain type of female. He was wearing a soiled, white coat, and looked all in. Taylor noticed particularly his small feet.

"You're Lee, aren't you?"

"What of it?"

"I'm Inspector Taylor from the Kimpton police. I want to see your employer, where would he be?"

"In the mating shed, behind the house."

"I shall want to see you too afterwards, where will you be?"

"In the barn; I've got a room in the corner. But I don't know anything if it's about Dottie."

"We'll see, shall we."

Mr and Mrs Woodman were both in the mating shed. It was hot in there and there was a faint, musky smell overlaid by a stronger smell of horses.

Both wore polo-necked sweaters under their white coats, and jodhpurs. Both were in their forties, both looked tired out, as had Lee.

Mrs Woodman was tall with a strong face, without make-up, well-built and with a faded prettiness. Taylor detected a trace of sadness in her eyes which were brown.

Woodman was tall as Taylor but broad with it, with a tanned face, a big hooked nose, and full lips, a man who could be attractive to some women. Both had greying hair, and Woodman inclined to baldness on top. In the fashion of long time horsemen he was slightly bow-legged and, Taylor thought, had surprisingly small feet.

Taylor produced his warrant card and introduced himself.

"I'm sorry to bother you when you're busy, but I have a few questions I'd like to ask."

"We're not busy any more, Inspector. We've just finished a first mating, not an easy task, and a delicate one. Jason, our stallion, is the star of the show although, unlike the film stars, he doesn't appear until the end. One of our old-timers is used to arouse the mare; poor old chap, he doesn't have any fun or reward.

"If you will wait indoors while my wife and I clean up I'll be pleased to answer your questions, if I can, although I did tell Sergeant Bennett this morning that we couldn't help if it was about the Shervell girl."

"This would be more about relationships, Sir."

"Come into the house then, we won't be long."

Taylor followed them into the mellow brick, two-storey house standing on its own. The buildings housing the stalls for the horses were spread out behind the mating shed.

He was shown into a small study with a coal fire burning brightly.

"Make yourself comfortable," Tessa Woodman said, "it's better than the church hall which is usually as cold as charity. Can I get you something?"

"Nothing, thank you Mrs Woodman."

There was a glass-fronted bookcase in one corner, a desk with a red ledger on it, and a shelf of books behind the desk. Taylor realised that running stables was a business like any other.

He rose when Woodman entered. He was still wearing the sweater but cord trousers now and slippers that looked like socks.

"Go ahead, Inspector."

"It's about Lee, Mr Woodman."

"He's invaluable, he loves horses, and he's fearless, even with the stallion when he's aroused, and it takes strength to hold Jason and guide him without doing any damage. The trouble is he plays on it, and he's far too impatient at times, today for example."

"How did you come to take him on, Sir?"

"When Matthew, an older man, retired I had to get someone quickly. We just have the one working stallion now but Jason has a fine pedigree and the stud side of the business is worth it because he's got a reputation and he's kept busy. But it's the riding horses and the stabling that pays, and it's hard work, too much for Tessa and I. There is more stabling beyond the block you saw, extending right up to the common land that separates it from the fencing enclosing the Devil's Ground..."

"Excuse me, Sir, the Devil's Ground?"

"I thought you might have heard about it by now. It's a stretch about a quarter of a mile square full of dene holes of unknown depths. It's also honeycombed with streams. In fact, the mill stream is said to have burst out of the ground, turning itself as it goes through Kimpton and into Yarborough as a fully fledged river, the Yar.

"The common land extends down as far as the back of the Old Rectory where it opens out into meadows as far along as Up Markham. We use them for rides and grazing. There are stands of trees which give shelter in hot weather for riders to have a break. It's frozen now, but there is a bridle path we can use for exercise. It's going to rain soon, though."

"As you said, Sir, a lot of work."

"Tessa helps me and Lee, and Rose Callender. Do you know her?"

"I have heard of her."

"In India she used to look after her husband's polo ponies. She misses them and she volunteered to help me out if required. She keeps two horses of her own in stables. She is also a great help in the stud, the mating. Having looked after horses, ponies if you like, she has as much strength as Lee. As a matter of fact I phoned her last night to ask if she would help out today, stand in for Lee, but there was no answer, and I called at least three times; it was unusual."

While Woodman was talking, without getting round to answering the questions as to why, and how, he had taken on Lee, Taylor was remembering Blackwell and his little nuggets of information which had not appeared yet. Woodman must have read his thoughts.

"I'm sorry, Inspector, I talk too much; comes of talking to horses who can't answer back. You were asking how did I come to get Lee.

"I was in Yarborough to see a colleague and friend, Alan Forrest, who runs a bigger spread than mine, and I mentioned that Matthew had left and I needed a replacement; incidentally, that's where Tessa and I were last night. We didn't get back till eleven, late for us, and as Tessa had a headache she went straight indoors and I did stables on my own. Lee was missing, and when I tackled him this morning he said he saw us coming and thought it would be alright if he went off to keep a date. Funny thing, I'm sure we saw Leask disappear into Reeves Alley as we were coming up Coopers Lane. I'm sorry, Inspector, I'm off again."

Taylor laughed politely.

"Anyway, Forrest was employing Lee but wanted to get rid of him. He had become over-familiar with some of the ladies who patronised Forrest, so much so that he had received complaints from husbands as well. He said he would be sorry to part with Lee because he was a natural. He wouldn't have the same opportunity for dalliance here so I decided to take him, and I've had only one complaint in two years, from Lesley Porritt. I bought a horse for her and she keeps it here. She said Lee was upsetting her by the way he used his hands when he was helping her to mount. I tore him off a strip and I've had no complaint since."

"What's his pedigree, Sir?"

"Forrest and I both think he's a gypsy. Probably why he and the girl got on so well, like attracted to like."

"You know the girl's history?"

"Everyone in Crowsett does."

"They were close, were they, Sir?"

"Yes."

"Engaged?"

"I haven't heard that."

"Have you any idea where Lee went last night?"

"I know he wasn't in the barn to keep his date because the light wasn't on."

"You allow him to have girls in the barn, Sir?"

"Yes. With his reputation I do not want him tomcatting round the village for his pleasure. I have an arrangement with him. He can have liaisons in the barn so long as he has the main light on when he's in there. And, there's a time limit. Last night, for example, when I came back from doing stables, the barn light was on. My bedroom (Tessa and I sleep separately, I'm a noisy sleeper), overlooks the barn, and when I came to bed the light was off."

"Thank you, Mr Woodman, for your help. The information you gave me will be a great help. Do you mind if I go into the barn to see

Lee, he did say he would be in there when I met him as I was coming in?"

"Not at all, Inspector,"

Taylor got up to go when Woodman said:

"Is Lee a suspect, Inspector?"

"At this early stage we are following certain leads, and if Lee and the dead girl were close, that could be a lead. I do also want to know whether he was telling the truth about his movements last night."

Taylor shook hands with Woodman and, leaving the house, crossed Coopers Lane and went into the barn.

Once inside he made for Lee's room which was over on the left, a continuation of a partition separating the outside wall and the 'false' wall which had been created to allow a small room to he constructed.

Lee was lying on the bed reading a paper back with a lurid cover.

"Do you mind if I sit down, Mr Lee?"

"Please yourself." Lee looked and sounded sullen. The gypsy strain was plain to see as Taylor studied him and his surroundings. The room was certainly spartan. A bed, a hanging wardrobe covered with a cloth, and a dressing chest. Attached to the back wall was a wash basin, and beside it a portable WC.

Taylor sat in the only chair in the room, a battered kitchen affair.

"How well did you know Dorothy Shervell?"

"We went out a few times." He didn't even bother to look up.

"Did you have her in here?"

Lee put down the book and there was an edge to his voice when he said:

"Who told you I did?"

"You didn't answer my question."

"I may have, but I didn't kill her."

"I didn't ask you if you did. Why so quick to deny it?"

Lee didn't answer.

"You were in trouble in Yarborough over a woman; were you in trouble with Dottie?"

"No."

"But you gave her a ring, you were engaged, her mother said so."

"If the old girl said that, she's a liar. Dottie bought the ring herself and made out it come from me because I didn't have enough money."

"Which means that you would have bought her one if you'd had the money."

"I didn't say that."

Lee had begun to sweat.

"You implied it. That ring was torn off her finger last night. Was it you taking it back after you'd killed her?"

"No, I didn't. I wasn't in the Shaw and I can prove it."

There was a lack of conviction in Lee's reply, his denial.

"Where were you?"

"Well," Lee hesitated, then hurried on, "I was in Kimpton and I went to the flicks and I met this bird. We mucked about a bit inside and then I said I'd walk home with her. We stopped in an alley and I thought I had it made but she said it was too cold and she ran off."

Lee was sweating even more now, and Taylor pressed on.

"How could you be in a cinema in Kimpton when you saw Mr and Mrs Woodman coming down Coopers Lane at eleven o' clock?"

"I lied. I didn't want Mr Woodman to think I'd left the horses unguarded."

"What was the girl's name?"

"I didn't ask her."

"Where does she live?"

"I don't know, she ran off."

"Where was the alley?"

"Some alley, I don't know where."

"What was the film you saw?"

"I didn't see much of it, a war film, I think!"

"You think, you think. You went to Kimpton, to the pictures. You were groping a bird, you walked home with her, only you stopped in an alley to have it off, only she ran off because it was too cold. You don't know what film, her name, where she lived, or what alley it was. It's a load of old cobblers, isn't it Lee?"

"It's not, it's true. You're supposed to take me to the station and warn me."

Lee was beginning to shake.

"You know all about that. Not yet. Let's continue. You must still have the ticket stub. You would have put it in your pocket. Where is it, in a suit hanging up there?"

"I threw it away."

Lee slumped in his chair, his head down.

"You threw it away; who are you kidding?"

Taylor let the silence develop before saying quietly:

"I shall come and see you again when I've got the reports of what was discovered in the Shaw."

"You won't find anything there!"

"Why anything?"

"I mean anything of mine."

Taylor looked long and hard at Lee until Lee looked down at his book.

"I'll be back."

Taylor got up swiftly and walked out. Lee had something to hide, Taylor was certain. He hadn't shown fear; anyone who could handle a randy stallion wouldn't be afraid. Apprehension, most likely; he had sweated. As he made his way down Coopers Lane and into Cowmeadow Lane, Taylor was certain he had his killer.

*****

It was just after three when Taylor knocked on the door of Kehoe's cottage. The door was opened by a man of medium height, painfully thin, sallow, with eyes of a neutral colour sunk in his head. He was wearing a dressing gown over a shirt and trousers and slippers.

Taylor introduced himself and was invited in. Close to, Taylor could see that Kehoe's hair was prematurely grey and must have been at one time reddish in colour. He smelt of drink, and if not already drunk, was well on the way to being so.

Kehoe led the way into what passed for a sitting room. It did not appear to have been cleaned for weeks, and unfinished paintings were propped up all round the skirting of one wall. It was freezing cold and there was a strong smell of whisky, although it was more like whiskey, Taylor thought, as he saw a bottle of 'JJ' on a trolley.

"You're just in time for a snort, Inspector. What'll it be, there's Jamieson's or a malt, what is your pleasure?"

"Nothing for me, thank you Sir."

"Sit down, Inspector, if you can find a space. You won't mind if I indulge, I'm sure."

Picking up the empty glass which stood next to the bottle, he half-filled it and took it to an old cane chair and placed it in a holder attached to the chair before sitting down.

He saw Taylor looking at the holder.

"Neat, isn't it, Inspector? My last link with India where I was sent for being a naughty boy. Cheers."

Half of the half he had put in the glass was downed in one swallow. He pulled an old blanket over his legs and sat back.

"It's cold, isn't it, and as usual I forgot to order any coal. Go ahead, Inspector, I suppose you've come in person about last night's affair which is the talk of the village by now. My information comes from a gabby neighbour. I do hope you're warm enough, these hovels weren't made for central heating."

If you listened you could detect the Irish accent.

"Why am I to be honoured by a second visit; I told the Sergeant I had nothing to offer?"

"Did you know the dead girl, Sir?"

Kehoe emptied the glass. His flippant manner disappeared and his tone was almost venomous as he replied.

"Did I know her, that little bitch, and I do speak ill of the dead. Everyone knew her for what she was. In addition to her other accomplishments, over which I shall draw a veil, she was probably old Alice's familiar, or possibly a witch herself."

"By Alice I assume you mean Mrs Shervell, but what is a 'familiar'?"

"A familiar, Inspector, is defined as being a demon, or demoness, attending on and obeying a witch. Of course, Dottie could have been a deputy or vice-witch."

"The witch being Mrs Shervell?"

"Of course. I can't make up my mind whether she'd be black or white, probably white. Dottie would, of course, be black.

You know Alice uses tarot cards. Do you know what they are?"

"Yes, I do. She's cunning enough to make money telling fortunes with them. There is a tinge of black in the rumour that she put a spell on her old man when he bolted to Shelbourne and got himself run over by a lorry."

"Isn't that a bit far-fetched, Sir?"

"Far from it, the history of Crowsett is bound up with witchcraft. The place was littered with witches and familiars at one time. Satanic rites were held in the Shaw, which had a different name then. And then, of course, there was Jane Corby..."

"I have heard of her, Sir."

"Well, she was, I mean Dottie was, a Corby on her and mother's side. Oh Inspector, you should see your face."

He began laughing which turned to coughing, and he went over to the trolley and refilled his glass.

"Thank you for the lecture, Sir, you must have good sources."

"None better, the Rector himself. He has copies of the parish records."

"Does he think Mrs Shervell is a witch, or her daughter?"

"I never asked him, but I hardly think he would believe it."

"I asked if you knew the girl and you said," Taylor looked at his notebook, "'she was a little bitch, as well as a familiar, or a witch herself.' Was that the extent of your knowledge of her, Mr Kehoe?"

Kehoe took another drink.

"Perhaps I should have confined myself to saying what she was to me. I felt, every time I saw her, that she could have made a meal of me, unattractive as I am. Do you know what I mean?"

"I think I do. You were saying that to you she was a good-time girl."

"Come off it, Inspector. She was a whore, pure and simple, although neither of those adjectives could possibly apply to her."

Taylor, thought it was time to change the subject.

"I believe you spent some time in India, you did say that, Sir?"

"I did. But what it has to do with the matter in hand escapes me."

"Just this, Sir, while you were in India did you have any knowledge of thuggee?"

"Thuggee! Good God! Thugs operated light years ago. They were put down in the 1800s I believe, although I suppose a Thug or two may have carried on after that. Why thuggee? Wait. Rumour has it, via my gabby neighbour, that the girl was strangled. You suspect thuggee? That's a bit much."

"Just a thought, Sir. The manner of the killing.

"Changing the subject, Sir, would you be acquainted with a Mr Leask?"

Kehoe's reaction was immediate. He appeared deeply angry, and his voice took on a softer Irish accent, more of the South than the North.

"Why ask that?"

"He was seen at about eleven last night coming out of Reeves Alley on his way back to Church Lane where he lives. I wondered if he had been to see you, unless, of course, he had other friends in this neighbourhood, which seems unlikely."

"As a matter of fact he was here. I was out when he came, and he let himself in. He wanted to talk about food, he is writing a new book and my cousin is a chef at The Shelburne in Dublin. I was a dab hand myself once, although you'd never guess it. He picked my brains, we talked, we argued, I was getting a headache again, and I wanted a drink; he doesn't drink, so he went."

"What time was that?"

"At eleven, I looked at the clock."

"My DC is seeing him now, Sir, or should be. No doubt he'll check when he knows we know he wasn't telling the truth."

"Don't bother him too much, Inspector. He's a sensitive fellow, and I wouldn't want him to get the wrong impression."

"My DC will see to that. Of course you won't tell him we discussed it. Then he might be offended!"

"I understand, Inspector, you're very kind."

"You've been very helpful, Mr Kehoe, and I'm grateful. It may be necessary to see you again, it may not."

*****

The Old Rectory stood in its own grounds almost opposite The Pilgrim's Rest. A gravel drive led up to the front door, and Blackwell was about to ring the bell when a girl appeared from the side of the house on the left. He stared as she joined him. She was indeed lovely as the Sergeant had said. Her fair hair was tied back with a wide, yellow ribbon, her jumper was pale blue and shapeless over a pale blue wool skirt, she had long, beautiful legs and her sandals were flat and of a neutral colour. Her eyes were as blue as the skirt, her nose finely shaped and her mouth generous. Clothing could not disguise the fact that she was as shapely as she was lovely. He came to when she said quite sharply:

"Please don't press the bell. My father worked late last night so he's taken a pill and gone back to bed."

Before he could reply she said:

"You're staring."

"I'm sorry. I'm Detective Constable Blackwell from Kimpton Police..."

The girl was trying to hide a smile. He replied as sharply as she had done.

"Did I say something funny?"

She reacted angrily.

"No, it's only that you don't look like a policeman."

"But I am, this is my warrant card." He held it out.

"Don't bother. If you want to ask questions you'll have to ask me. We'd better go into the kitchen, please follow me."

She led him round to the side of the house and into the kitchen. It was enormous. One of the windows looked out on to the road, the other into the back garden. All round the walls were copper-coloured pans hanging on hooks. There were three tables, two large and one small, and a massive electric stove with a glass front.

On the smaller table a rack of scones gave out a wonderful smell which made his mouth water. The girl saw him looking at them.

"Will you stop being angry if I offer you a scone, I've not long made them, but I think they've cooled enough?" She smiled.

"I'd love one," and he smiled back.

"Would you like butter and strawberry jam, I made that myself?"

"Yes to both. Can I help?"

"If you'd like coffee you could make it; it's instant and decaffeinated, Father won't have any other. It's in the cupboard, plenty of saucepans for the milk which is in the fridge."

That was round a corner and was as big as the stove.

With the coffee made and the scone ready on a plate with a paper serviette, Blackwell sat down while the girl stood over a mixing bowl, her coffee beside her on one of the big tables.

"I'm making a cake. Carry on with your questions. By the way, don't think all this you see is ours. We're renting the house from the church commissioners and everything came with it."

"I'm sorry I was rude," Blackwell confessed, "but I do get tired of people saying I don't look like a policeman."

"I'm sorry too. I expect your questions are about Dorothy. What a terrible thing to happen in this lovely village. Have you any clues?"

"Nothing at present, that's why we're interviewing anyone who had dealings with the girl. Would I be rude if I said how brown you were?"

She laughed.

"No. It's left over from India, I expect. I was born there and lived there until six years ago. It only takes a ride in the fresh air, even in the winter, to bring it out again."

"Were you sorry to leave?"

"Very sorry. We had to. Father worked for the British Government and one day he spoke rather sharply to a member of the ruling congress party. We had to leave at a moment's notice, and now we are persona something. We stayed in London with my aunt for a short while, but Father wanted to come home, having been born in this house. We were able to rent it because the Rector is a bachelor and didn't want it."

"Was your grandfather a Rector here?"

"And great grandfather. In the garden you can see a summer house, it revolves so that it can follow the sun. Three generations used to write their sermons in there."

"Why didn't your father want to follow his father as Rector?"

"Father says they quarrelled about the high church, some disagreement."

"I'd better start the questions now. How well did you know Dorothy?"

"I suppose as well as anybody else in Crowsett; she was a mystery. I helped her because she needed work, she said, and she came on three afternoons to help me with the cleaning. A lot of the rooms aren't used but they still have to be cleaned. I gave her things, she told such a tale that I felt sorry for her. And she paid me back by stealing. Little things at first, finally Father's gold watch. He treasured it; it was a present when he retired and it was engraved inside. It was in a bureau in the sitting room and fortunately he went for some paper in there and found it gone. He told her to get out and said that he would tell the Sergeant, which he did. Mr Bennett never found it although he searched the cottage where she lived."

"What about her friends?"

"I don't know that she had any female friends..."

"You know of her reputation?"

"I was made aware of it very early on."

"Was she linked with anyone special?"

"The only one I heard of was Lee, the groom who works at the stables. I have a horse which I keep there, my Charlie, my only luxury, and I ride. My friend is Rose Callender, have you met her yet?"

"I shall be seeing her, I expect."

"I must put my cake in the oven now, then I can sit down.

"Now, what were we saying?"

"About riding and Rose Callender."

"She has two horses and she helps Stephen, Stephen Woodman, quite a lot. She's very strong; she used to look after her husband's polo ponies in India. I told her that Lee was being too familiar and she called it wandering hands. I told Stephen and he put a stop to it. He's a menace, Lee I mean."

"Did you know that they were engaged?"

"I didn't know that. People said they were very close."

"Did Lee get familiar with Mrs Callender?"

"He couldn't have done, she would have told me."

"Do you get out very much?"

"What is there to get out for? Crowsett is a backwater now that the younger people have all gone to the towns. It used to be fun although I could never see much of it because I type the book father is writing, and that keeps me occupied most of the time."

"I have to ask you where you and your father were at 11 p.m. last night?"

"Is that when she was killed?"

"We think so."

"Father was working, most of the night. I went to bed at ten-thirty and I was worried when I hadn't heard him come to bed after, I suppose, twenty or thirty minutes, so I went to his study, it's on the same floor as the bedrooms, and I listened. I heard him muttering to himself, which he does when he's writing, and I went back to bed."

"Just one thing more. You and your father were in India for a long time, did you know anything about thuggee?"

"What a question. Oh, I see why; the paper boy said Dorothy was strangled. Father would know more than I do, which is nothing. He has a chapter scheduled on cults, and thuggee was a cult, and a religion as well, according to his grandfather."

"Thank you for your help, Miss Porritt. And thank you, too, for the scone and the coffee."

"Which you made." They both laughed.

"Do you ever get into Kimpton?"

"Maybe once a fortnight, to go to Tesco's, it's much cheaper than Mr Hayhoe in the High Street, but then it can afford to be. Why?"

"I just thought that if you were there, and we happened to meet, we might have a coffee or a drink."

"Now you are not behaving like a policeman. Ought you to fraternise with a suspect?"

"You're quite right, maybe some other time."

"Maybe. Goodbye Mr Blackwell, sorry, Detective Constable Blackwell."

"Goodbye Miss Porritt."

*****

Blackwell was amazed when he looked at his watch. It was a quarter to four and meant that any further interviews were out of the question if Taylor's timetable was to be observed. He arrived at the church hall just on four o'clock and found Taylor fuming. He was angrier still when Blackwell told him he had completed one interview only with Lesley Porritt.

"What the hell were you doing. Don't tell me, you didn't see Porritt so you made do with the lovely Miss Porritt. You did say lovely, didn't you Wiggy?"

"Very lovely." Bennett looked at Blackwell and winked.

"You were right, Inspector, Mr Porritt wasn't available because he'd been working late and had taken a pill and gone back to bed.

I had to draw her out and it was a lengthy business because she covered quite a lot of ground. Two things of importance, both concerning Rose Callender. First, she has great strength, probably from looking after her husband's polo ponies in India, and also from the work she does for Woodman in the stud side of his business. Lee was over familiar..."

"I know that part, Woodman told me," Taylor interrupted.

"What I was going to say is that Miss Porritt told me that Rose Callender had not complained about his overfamiliarity with her. It might be significant bearing in mind her possible association with Lee. You know about Dorothy stealing, but Miss Porritt did not know they were engaged.

"Finally, I asked about thuggee. Her father is writing a book about India and has a chapter scheduled on thuggee, which she said is a cult as well as a religion.

"They are in no way suspects according to their movements last night."

"Not an awful lot of little nuggets, but at least we don't have to bother with them anymore.

It's just as well that you didn't see Leask and Mrs C. Leask was with Kehoe last night. He was shaken when I asked him if he had been and told me a load of rubbish. I think he and Leask are gay. I hate that word, it used to mean something happy until it was collared by the media, that's another lousy expression.

"Rose C. has something to hide too. Woodman said he tried to get in touch with her last night, several times, by phone, but there was no answer which he said was most unusual."

"Handle them both with kid gloves."

"Would it be better if you saw them?"

"No, I trust you to handle it. You've learned enough now to handle any interviews."

"Thanks, Inspector."

"I'm only hoping that the forensic reports will be in when I get back to the station. I squeezed Lee until he sweated. His alibi for last night stinks. He didn't wait for the Woodmans to come back but went, he says, to Kimpton to the flicks. There he met a bird and groped her before starting to take her home, stopping in an alley to have it off, only for her to run off because it was too cold..."

Bennett was roaring with laughter.

"He didn't know what the film was, he didn't know the girl's name or where she lived, and he didn't know where the alley was. Oh yes, and he threw his ticket stub away.

"I think he waited until he saw the Woodmans come back at about a quarter to eleven and scarpered up to the Shaw to keep his date with Dottie, taking the rope with him. But does a motive of wanting to better himself with Rosie stand up?"

"I must be off. While I'm away put your stuff with the Porritt girl on the recorder. The PCs won't be wanted any more so you can take them back, Wiggy, when you collect Blackwell's things from his flat. I'm sure one of us will be able to make a toasted sandwich."

"One of us can make a toasted sandwich alright, but it won't be Buck. I don't know the first thing about toasted sandwiches, do you Blackie?"

"No. Let's go and ask Parker."

Having had the Tefal toaster demonstrated to them, Bennett and Blackwell together with the two PCs left for Kimpton after putting a notice on the front door of the hall as Bennett had suggested.

He dropped the PCs off at the station and waited while Blackwell collected the things he would need for his stay at Up Markham. They were back at Bennett's cottage by six.

Joan Bennett was pleased to have Blackwell as a temporary guest, and took him upstairs and showed him his room.

Blackwell thought that she was a perfect foil to Bennett. Petite, very pretty, with an unwrinkled skin and good bone structure.

"I hope you like lamb, Blackie, may I call you Blackie?"

"I love it. With no disrespect to your cooking, I could eat a horse, Mrs Bennett."

"Joan, please."

"Joan."

Downstairs, Joan said to her husband:

"I have to go out tonight, love, Sally Croft is very near her time and I promised I'd look in in case it comes before the midwife does. So if you don't mind we'll have dinner a bit earlier. I'll go and get on with it."

"Any help wanted?"

"I can manage, you two have a drink, but no rum, leave that till later." They drank sherry before dinner which was simple but beautifully cooked and presented. Lamb chops, broccoli, peas and creamed potatoes, with onion gravy, followed by apple pie, with a crust that fell to pieces, and ice cream.

"Joan, may I say that that was a feast."

She coloured. "I'm so glad, I did work at it knowing you were coming."

"Would it be alright..." Blackwell looked at Bennett.

"Wiggy, but not when Taylor's about."

"Wiggy, if we asked Joan if we could do the washing-up?"

"Why Blackie," she looked at Bennett, "what a wonderful idea, you were dying to do it, weren't you, dear?"

"Of course, it's a splendid idea, isn't it?"

44

Joan laughed.

"Thank you, Blackie. At least I think it's a good idea."

After Joan had gone the two men sat down before the fire with a glass of rum each and lit up their pipes.

"This rum is the real stuff, Blackie. I managed to get a couple of bottles when they scrapped the issue. We'll never taste its like again."

"You and the Inspector go back a long way, Wiggy?"

"Back to when we were boys. Buck was born in Kimpton so we didn't meet until I had to go to the primary school at Kimpton. I remember we had a fight over something and he won. After that we were friends. At eleven he got a place at the grammar and I went to the secondary, but we were still pals. He could have gone on to university but when he heard I was joining the Navy he came too. My Dad was in the Navy, you see, and lost both legs when his ship was torpedoed. In my second year he died. It killed my mother, and she followed six months later. My older brother stayed on in the house and I was able to come home on leave until he died too, in a train crash. He wasn't married so I had the solicitor sell the house and bank the money.

"After that we spent our leave in the 'smoke', that's what we called London. We liked it so much that when our twelve was up we joined the Met. We were both married a year later, and both our wives were called Joan. My Joan was told she could never have a child or it would kill her so she took a job at a children's hospital. When I said we were moving back here I expected her to explode but she came like a lamb. She spends a lot of time at a crèche at Down Markham. She's always helping someone." He put his pipe down and sipped his rum.

"But Buck, three years ago, he phoned to tell me his Joan was expecting. He was over the moon. But when her time was nearly come some drunken bastard knocked her down and killed her in Lewisham High Road in a stolen car. They called Buck but by the time he reached the hospital she was dead."

"Did they get the fellow?"

"They got him alright. Some conscientious citizen followed the bloke and rang the police on his mobile phone.

"At his trial the bastard cried in the dock and said how sorry he was and it was really the lady's fault because she had walked out in front of him, and what with that and the smart brief he had, all he got was community service.

"I thought Buck would go out of his skull. I asked him to come and stay with us but he wouldn't. You see, it's the name Joan that puts him off. But he did transfer when he heard there was an opening here. His folks are dead and he lives on his own. People think he's a hard man, they certainly knew he was in the Met., but he's not when you get to know him."

"Why Wiggy and Buck?"

"That's what we were called in the Navy. Tallies, they're known as. You see, all Bennetts were Wiggy, and all Taylors were Buck. Like all Whites were called Chalky; all Youngs, Brigham; and all Palmers, Pedlar.

"More rum, Blackie?"

"No thanks, Wiggy, I won't need rocking tonight."

"Would you like to go up; I'll wait for Joan, I always do."

"Would she mind, would you mind?"

"Not at all, old lad. Good night."

"Good night."

*****

While Bennett and Blackwell were enjoying themselves, Taylor was facing Chief Superintendent Bloxham across Bloxham's desk.

"How is it going, Inspector?"

"We've made a start, Sir, and I have a suspect!"

"I'm sure that you will find something to help you in these reports."

He handed them to Taylor.

"May I read them now, Sir?"

"Go ahead."

Taylor began reading and when he had finished banged the desk in front of him.

"Help isn't strong enough, Sir, they are a lifeline. These put my suspect firmly in the frame. The girl was pregnant, the rope is from a stable, traces of straw in the weave, the weave, Blackwell said, probably custom-made, so easy to trace, and the damage done to the girl's neck, all point to someone connected with horses, and my suspect's employer spoke of the suspect's strength when dealing with a mating between a stallion and a mare, which would be enough to cause the damage that was done.

"He's an amateur, of course, or he wouldn't have left the rope, but cunning enough to leave no prints."

"Who is your suspect, Inspector?"

"A stable hand employed by Stephen Woodman who was engaged to the girl. The ring that was torn off her finger was the ring he gave her, Blackwell learned that from the girl's mother."

"You are allowing Blackwell to conduct interviews?"

"I have to, Sir, because of the time element. But I would do anyway because I trust him as I would myself. He shows great promise."

"Very well, so long as you are satisfied. Go on."

"Now that we have a motive there are others we should interview. The Doctor mentioned the possibility of thuggee."

"In Crowsett, that little village?"

"I know, Sir, but there are four people who have strong connections with India and I considered it advisable to explore every possibility,"

"Excellent, Inspector. I wonder if you could find time tonight to pay a visit to the hospital. DCI Brotherhood has had his operation and is naturally disappointed that he can take no part in the investigation. Bring him up to date"

"Yes Sir, yes Sir, three bags full, Sir," Taylor said to himself as he left.

Tuesday, March 28th

Bennett and Blackwell were already waiting in the church hall when Taylor came into the office with a broad smile on his face. He sat down and opened his briefcase.

"Exhibit No. 1," he said, producing the noose which Bloxham had given him before he left. "Exhibits two and three," as he produced the two reports.

"We now have the best motive in the world for murder; Dorothy Shervell was pregnant, and the doctor confirms that her Adam's apple, only he doesn't call it that, was crushed.

"The contents of her stomach were analysed and, helped by the information we gave him, the time of death is reckoned to be 11 p.m., twenty-three hundred hours, give or take ten minutes either side.

"The other forensic report is negative regarding prints, but they do say that the rope was custom-made, well done, Blackwell, and that there were, wait for it, minute traces of straw in the weave."

"And that puts Lee firmly in the frame," Bennett said.

"We'll see. Don't forget we have some more interviews added on to those carried forward from yesterday.

"I'll be taking the noose with me to show to Woodman, Lee and Kehoe. I want Woodman to identify it as one of his and we're well on the way when I go on to see Lee.

"Blackwell, I want you to see Mrs Callender first, then Leask. When you've finished come and join me where I'll be waiting to see Kehoe. I want you on your way to check the time it would have taken Leask to leave Kehoe and be seen by Flora Whatsit. Of course it'll be in reverse, but it should be enough to check how much time Kehoe had to get up to the Shaw, if he did, and do Dottie. Right?"

"Right, Inspector."

"Wiggy, you still haven't seen the Rector."

"No, he was out yesterday. I'll go this morning!"

"Do you think Kehoe would have had the strength to inflict that amount of damage on Dottie?"

"He's Irish, Blackwell, and he may very well be putting on an act. As for his drinking, with all he took when I was last with him, he could still talk quite normally."

"What about the rope, Buck?"

"People have made it plain that this village is so safe that no-one locks their doors. Kehoe told me that Leask walked straight in when he was out. That barn is so old that I doubt if it could be locked."

"I'll be on my way then to see Mrs Callender."

"And I'll be on my way to see the Rev."

"What is this?"

"Following instructions, Inspector," Bennett said and laughed.

Blackwell had only a short way to go the White House which stood almost on the corner of Church Lane in the High Street.

Mrs Callender answered his ring on the bell.

"You must be Mr Blackwell, the one who does not look like a policeman, so Lesley said, and she was right. Come in please."

Blackwell followed her into a large lounge full of heavy old and expensive furniture. The paintings round the walls and over the fireplace were of country scenes, including some of the village; none of them were prints or copies. The curtains at the big bay windows looking out on to the garden at the back were of heavy damask with tassels and pulls. There was a bright fire burning in the grate with a log on the top scenting the room. However, it could not mask the heavier perfume worn by Rose Callender. There were two large easy chairs either side of the fireplace, and next to one of them was a large, expensive television set with a shelf underneath holding a video recorder.

"Please take off your coat and make yourself comfortable while I make some tea; you do like tea?"

"Yes, thank you Mrs Callender."

He hadn't expected her to speak English so well. Her consonants were clipped, it was true, but there was an absence so far of the ubiquitous 'you know' favoured by many Anglo-Indians.

It was hot, and he did take his coat off.

He rose when Mrs Callender came in with the tea, or rather carrying a tray with a complete silver tea service and two bone china (he was sure) cups and saucers. He took the tray from her.

"This was much too heavy for you to carry, why didn't you call me?"

He put the tray down next to her chair. There was a similar small table next to his chair.

"I wanted to show off. It is beautiful, isn't it?"

"And worth a great deal, I hope it's insured."

"It is not necessary in Crowsett," she paused, "I was about to say, no crime, but that is not so now, is it?"

"No, I'm afraid not. That is why I wanted to ask you a few questions."

He waited until she had poured the tea, and took it back to his table.

"I didn't put any sugar in; it's a habit because I don't have any."

"This will be fine. May I begin?"

"Of course."

While she had been busy with the tea ceremony he had studied her. She had beauty, dark beauty, but he searched for an adjective to express the flaw which prevented it from being outright beauty. He could only think of his father's description of one of his favourite roses, 'full-blown', in the sense that she was too fully developed. She was overburdened with jewellery, with bracelets, gold and silver, on both wrists, gold earrings, and a heavy gold necklace.

"Do you wish to smoke?"

"No, I only smoke a pipe when I'm on my own." Which was a lie.

"What a pity, I love the smell of a pipe. My pater smoked one, and so did my husband, Charles, my late husband.

"My pater was a senior officer employed by the Indian Railways, he was Head of Signalling."

"Are you sorry you left India?"

"Yes and no. I promised Charles when he died that I would not let this house be sold, so I came to live here. Charles was only fifty years old but it was his heart. He played a lot of polo which is very strenuous. He had a stable of beautiful ponies; I looked after them; I played myself sometimes.

"Do you like your tea? It is from Assam; I have it sent to me."

"Very nice, I like it." Another lie. He favoured Twining's English Breakfast.

"Now, are you ready for a few questions?"

"Fire away."

"How well did you know the dead girl, Dorothy Shervell?"

"Why on earth should I have known her, that girl. I knew of her, who didn't, but know her, of course not."

Blackwell thought she protested a little too much.

"You ride a lot, Mrs Callender. Miss Porritt told me you ride together, and that Mr Woodman looks after your horses."

"That's right, Lesley is my friend. Do you not think she is lovely, Mr Blackwell?"

"Yes, very pretty. You would, therefore, have contact with the fellow Lee who works for Woodman."

"Yes, he looks after my horses. Why do you ask?"

"Miss Porritt had cause to report him to Mr Woodman for overfamiliarity. Did you find him overfamiliar?"

"No."

Sharp and abrupt: she was either really angry or rattled.

"Miss Porritt said that when she told you, you referred to his overfamiliarity as 'wandering hands'.

"I might have done. Are these questions really necessary? I told the Sergeant this morning, no, yesterday morning, that I could not help with his enquiry, and now you bring in Joseph."

"Joseph?"

"That is his name, one cannot call him 'Lee' all the time."

"He has been out with you in your car, I understand."

"That is a lie. Who told you that, Stephen?"

"Stephen?"

"Stephen Woodman. He and his wife Tessa own the stables. He does not like me. I must tell you, in confidence Mr Blackwell, that Mr Woodman made advances to me which I repulsed, and so he does not like me. I am very sorry for Tessa, his wife.

"I do not think he likes Joseph either."

"Why would that be?"

"You should ask him."

"Having a great knowledge of India as you must have, Mrs Callender, would you know very much about thuggee?"

"Thuggee?"

"There was an element about the killing of the girl that made the Doctor who examined her mention a similarity to thuggee"

"I see. We all knew about the religion, or cult, if you wish. Pater had records telling of how the Thugs would even travel on the trains and kill, for Kali the Goddess, they said, but more likely for money."

"Only one more question, Mrs Callender. Mr Woodman told the Inspector that he telephoned you on Sunday night to ask if you would help with a first mating the following morning because he was afraid that Lee would be too hasty, and although he telephoned several times there was no reply, which was unusual."

"Sunday night," she mused, "Ah yes, I remember now. I was watching an Asian film, which I had recorded, on the small television in my bedroom. I have Sky television; there is a dish, is that right, dish..."

"Yes, it is."

"On the side of the house, and I have a special card to watch the Asian programmes. Billy Woodnutt showed me how to record the programme which is usually very late so that I can see it when I like.

"I have no telephone extension upstairs. If I am watching or asleep, I do not wish to be disturbed."

"I understand, Mrs Callender. Thank you for being so patient and so helpful. Goodbye."

"Goodbye."

His next visit was to Leask, again only a short distance away. Leask was much as he had imagined him to be although his plumpness did not show up on the head and shoulder photographs which appeared on the back of his books. But he wasn't fat. He was shortish, a smooth, unlined skin, hair, thinning, brushed across the top of his head to conceal incipient baldness, and very red, very full lips.

He was wearing a silken jacket, elaborately decorated, over grey trousers, and red velvet slippers matching the colour in the jacket. Blackwell had his warrant card ready as Leask opened the front door. "Detective Constable Blackwell, Mr Leask, could I ask you a few questions?"

"Another policeman, and don't you mean more questions? The sergeant questioned me yesterday, and I told him I knew nothing about the girl or the murder. I suppose you'd better come in."

Leask's sitting room was also at the back looking out on to a fence separating his bungalow from the Rector's. The main colour throughout the room was yellow. There was some chinoiserie, small vases and one big standing vase, all beautifully decorated. There were paintings around the walls except over the fireplace where there was a space.

"Sit down, Mr... err.?"

"Blackwell, Sir."

"I saw you looking round; do you admire the room?"

"It's very pleasant, Sir, and if you don't mind me saying, exceptional for a small bungalow in a village like Crowsett.

"I take that as a compliment. It's odd that you should say that. I have an apartment in New York and a flat in London with similar decor, and yet I was born in a village exactly like this one, in Kent. My father was a shopkeeper, a gentleman's outfitter. How did I become involved with food? It was my mother who taught me not only to love good food, but also how to cook it. I was lucky.

"I came here because I took a wrong turning on my way back from Paul's Bay where there is a first-class hotel on which I was reporting. I saw the church, and churches fascinate me, so I stopped and saw this bungalow which was for sale. I bought it. I'm sorry but you did get me talking. Ask your questions."

"Mr Leask, you told Sergeant Bennett yesterday that on Monday night you went to the post box in the High Street to post a chapter of your new book to your publisher in London. You did say that?"

"Yes I did. Why?"

"Because, with all due respect, Sir, it wasn't true, was it?"

"You don't accept my word?"

"I'm afraid not, Sir. You see, when the box was opened there was no packet or letter in there which could have contained what you said.

In fact, you were seen at 11 p.m. leaving Reeves Alley, crossing the High Street, and meeting the Rector at the corner of this lane, when you disappeared up the lane together."

"Who the devil told you that?"

"Does it matter, Sir? Is it true?"

"Aha! Reeves Alley is next to the wool shop run by the village gossip, Flora Poste. It was that woman, wasn't it? She should be run out."

"But that is what happened, isn't it Sir?"

"Alright, I lied. I had been to see someone whom I would rather not name because it wouldn't reflect any credit on me. Is there anyone else in that area who has been interviewed?"

"There is Mr Woodman at the stables, and, oh yes, a Mr Kehoe..."

"That's the man I went to see..."

Leask's relief was apparent.

"I was reluctant to name him because he is a drunkard. But he is a very good painter when he likes to be and sometimes finishes a painting. That's why I went to see him. There is, as you can see, an empty space over the fireplace, and I wished to commission a painting of the church and the two bungalows.

I arrived at his cottage, in the road with the awful name..."

"Cowmeadow Lane, Sir."

"That's right. He wasn't in..."

"What time was that, Sir?"

"A quarter to ten. Do you see this watch..."

He pulled up his cuff, and Blackwell would describe it later as having everything on it except the kitchen sink.

"It does not lose a second in a year, possibly longer. Kehoe was out so I went in and waited. It was almost as cold inside as it was outside. He had been for a walk to clear his head. I should think it needed it. It was ten-fifteen. We talked and he agreed to do the painting. We also talked about food; a cousin of his is a chef at The Shelburne in Dublin and Kehoe passes on a few tips to me. I left at exactly ten forty-five."

"You're certain that it was ten forty-five, Sir?"

"Having seen my watch do you doubt my word?"

"No. Thank you Mr Leask, you have been very helpful."

Blackwell made his way back to Cowmeadow Lane, walking at the pace Leask would most likely adopt.

*****

Taylor was invited in to see Woodman, and once inside the study he opened his briefcase and produced the noose.

"Good God, man, was that round her neck. It's so small."

"It is, Mr Woodman, and I've brought it here for a purpose. Do you think you could handle it? Forensic say that it could be custom-made and that it had traces of straw in the weave. What I want to know, is whether it could have been a piece taken from one of the ropes made for you." Woodman opened a drawer in the bureau and took out a magnifying glass. He looked carefully and closely at the noose. Straightening up, he said:

"It is from one of ours, I know by the weave and the colours in it. The ropes my man makes are all different when it comes to the weave. It's part of a head collar we use for horses, for leading them. It's one we would have discarded, it's worn and it's stretched. That makes the strands weaken."

"Where would it have been kept, Mr Woodman?"

"In the barn, out of the way, in one of the bins. It could only be used in an emergency."

"Thank you very much, Mr Woodman. Could I have the name of your supplier?"

Woodman wrote the name and address on a sheet of note paper and passed it to Taylor.

"Does this look bad for Lee?"

"At the moment I have an open mind, Sir. Where is he, in the barn?"

Woodman looked at his watch.

"Yes, he'll be there for the next half-hour."

They shook hands again and Taylor went out into Coopers Lane and across to the barn. Lee was sitting on the bed in the same position as before, reading.

"Something for you to look at instead of that rubbish."

Taylor threw the noose on to the bed beside Lee.

"What do I want with that thing?"

"You don't know; I'm surprised. It was taken off Dottie's neck. See the blood on it, and notice the weave. It had straw in it. Your boss tells me that it was cut from a piece of rope that was kept in here."

Lee threw it back.

"It's got nothing to do with me," he almost shouted, and Taylor could see that at last he was frightened.

"You can't pin anything on me," Lee almost shouted again. "I wasn't nowhere near the Shaw, I was in Kimpton."

"So you said, at the cinema, only you didn't know the name of the film, or the name of the girl you groped, or where she lived, or what alley you stopped in, and to cap it all, you threw your cinema ticket stub away. And you say one thing about waiting until the Woodmans came home and going to the cinema, which wouldn't be easy at eleven p.m."

"So I lied. I went after they went to Yarborough."

"And risked leaving a stableful of horses to go chasing a skirt when you could have had one in the barn. Oh yes, Mr Woodman told me that too."

Lee didn't answer.

"And surprise, surprise, Dottie was going to have your kid."

Lee did look up then.

"It wasn't mine, she told me she was going to have one, but it wasn't mine."

"Whose was it?"

"I don't know, probably one of the darts team."

"The darts team were at Shelbourne from six-thirty until two Monday morning.

Be fair to yourself, Joe, it's Joe isn't it. Get it off your chest. We can be understanding. But unless you come clean I'm going to do tomorrow what you wanted me to do, take you down to the station. If you do want to talk tonight DC Blackwell will be staying with

Sergeant Bennett. Phone him, the number will be on a paper attached to the door of the church hall."

Taylor left him, knowing well that he had gone as far, maybe farther, than he should have done without taking him down to the station for questioning. But he was certain he had his man; one more push and he'd fold up. The question was would it be tonight or tomorrow at the station.

Blackwell was waiting for him at the bottom of Coopers lane.

"The time Leask would have taken would have been right, he's probably a slow walker, but he didn't leave Kehoe at eleven, he left at a quarter to."

"How did you get him to say he was with Kehoe?"

"He practically volunteered it. He dithered a bit and than asked if we had been to see anyone else in the area. When I mentioned Woodman and then Kehoe he pounced on it. Put Kehoe wouldn't like to know what his friend said about him. He, Leask, hadn't liked to mention his visit because Kehoe was a drunkard, and it would not reflect any credit on himself..."

Taylor was laughing.

"Go on," he said, "I hope there's more."

"Not much. He said he went to see Kehoe about a painting, and they talked also about food because Kehoe has a cousin..."

"I know, at The Shelburne in Dublin. You did well. You weren't putting me on, were you?"

"It was the truth, believe me."

"Right. You can go back to the hall now, this won't take me long."

Kehoe opened the door and it looked as if he had slept, if he did, in the same clothes as he had worn before.

"Good morning, Inspector. Come in and don't have a drink."

If possible the sitting room was in a worse mess than before. Kehoe settled himself in his chair holding a full glass of whiskey.

Taylor took out the noose from his briefcase and held it up.

"This..." he started to say, but Kehoe was out of his chair, hand over his mouth, heading for the nether regions of his cottage. Taylor heard him being very sick. Fortunately, before his departure, he had had the sense to put the full glass in the holder attached to his chair.

When he returned his face was a pale green and he almost fell into his chair. He picked up the glass, sipping before replacing it.

"That was a foul thing to do, Inspector, without warning. It is, isn't it?"

"Yes, Mr Kehoe."

Kehoe echoed what Woodman had said, "It's so small."

"The girl was pregnant."

"Are you telling me that, and showing me that, that thing, for a reason?"

"Mr Leask says that he left you at a quarter to eleven, not eleven."

"You've seen him? How did my name come into it?"

"My detective constable saw him. You see, Sir, Mr Leask had told Sergeant Bennett a lie when he was seen on Monday morning. He said he had been to post something to his publisher in London. There was no mail for London in the box, so we had to check where he had been. He hedged a bit and then admitted he had been to see you about a painting he wanted to commission."

"Good for him!"

Taylor wondered what he would have said if he knew what Leask had really said as well.

"As a matter of fact, Inspector, he did leave at a quarter to. My clock was fifteen minutes fast, I noticed it this morning, and as you see, it is now correct.

"Is that all Michael said?"

"Well, he did say some other things which I won't repeat."

"About me?"

"Indirectly and directly, Mr Kehoe. But nothing was said to him that could have upset him."

"You intrigue me. Knowing what a devious bugger you are I have to believe you for telling the truth once, that's an Irish way of putting it."

"I won't keep you any longer, Mr Kehoe. I hope that it won't be necessary to see you again, but it has been illuminating to talk with you."

"And I with you, Mr Taylor. I wish you success in your search for the girl's killer: she may have been a bad 'un but she didn't deserve that fate."

On his return to the church hall Bennett greeted him with the news that the Rector would speak only to him.

"Hell! What time is it, my watch has stopped?"

"Nearly twelve, Inspector. Toasted sandwich and coffee for you?"

"Anything, Blackwell. When I come back I've got to sort this lot out, and hear from you about Rosie C."

The Rector was dressed in a track suit when he answered the door. "Come in, Inspector. I'm in the process of composing a sermon for Sunday that will reflect on the evil which has hit our village."

When they were seated he said, "I did lie, a white lie, although clergymen should not be allowed to tell any sort of lie. A lady is concerned, hence the necessity for it."

"I'm sorry, Sir, I quite understand."

"No you do not, Inspector, not with that look on your face. The lady and I happen to be engaged, and will be married later this year. As I shall be leaving the parish afterwards I would not wish that information broadcast."

"I do understand, Sir."

"I was with the old lady in Mill Lane until eight-thirty and walked over the hill to Shackleford where the lady lives. I stayed until ten-fifteen and walked slowly back. I have a pulled muscle in one leg which slows me up especially when it's cold."

"Playing sport Sir? I did notice the photograph."

"Yes. That was taken in my last term at the Carnegie PT College. I became a schoolmaster before I was ordained."

"As a matter of interest, Sir, in our interviews with various people in the village there has been talk of a Jane Corby. Apparently the dead girl fancied she was a reincarnation of her. Was there such a person, and is there any possibility of it being true, not that I think there is."

"I expect most of your information comes from Mrs Shervell..."

"And Mr Kehoe."

"Ah, Mr Kehoe. Let's deal with him later. Mrs Shervell was, I know, deeply worried about Dorothy, and came to me for help and advice. I did my best, but all that you have heard is true, except the possibility of reincarnation, although there are astonishing similarities in the statistics of the two girls, namely dates of birth and death and age, both were twenty-two when they died.

"Mr Kehoe has a fertile imagination, but he is, by and large, a very intelligent man, and one I feel very sorry for because his life was ruined by his dismissal from Trinity College in Dublin, and subsequent failure to make good in India.

"He came seeking information about early times in Crowsett and I was able to allow him to examine the old parish records, wonderfully preserved by Mr Porritt, the present Mr Porritt's father, when he was Rector. At the start of the last war he buried them in the grounds in a stout iron box. It was just as well for a bomb, jettisoned from a German aeroplane being chased by British fighters, destroyed all but the lych-gate.

"It was a miracle, you might say, that there, under the lych-gate, rested the crew of that German plane which was shot down near Shackleford, before they were buried in the cemetery.

"This is, in fact, the third St Dominic's church, two in the past were burned down by satanists.

"Kehoe loves to air his knowledge of the early days here, and who should criticise him for it?"

"Why Rector, Sir?"

"That dates back to the days when the incumbent relied on tithes, tenths of all produce, which were placed in the tithe barn."

"Thank you very much, Sir. I wish I had more time to listen to you but I must get on. You have been very helpful, and your secret is safe with me."

"Thank you Inspector. I should be very happy to see you again."

*****

"It all fits," Taylor said, as the three men sat in the office at the church hall having finished their meal.

"Woodman confirmed that the rope had come from one of his old head collars which were kept in the barn to be used only in an emergency.

"Lee was scared out of his skull, but he didn't break although he was almost there. I left him with the promise that I would have him down at the station tomorrow unless he came through with something tonight I told him there would be a notice on the outside door with your number on it, Wiggy.

"Let's hear what Rosie had to say, Blackwell."

"What did you think of her, Blackie?"

"Overpowering; attractive, if you like a woman who uses too much perfume and is loaded down with jewellery: bracelets galore, gold, of course; well spoken.

"Points: she said that Lee being in her car was a lie and was probably said by Woodman who didn't like her because he made a pass at her and was repulsed, her expression, not mine. He probably doesn't like Lee either. When I asked why, she said 'ask him'. But she did get rattled and referred to 'Joseph'. When I asked who Joseph was she said, 'You can't keep calling him Lee'.

"The only other thing was about horses. She and Lesley Porritt are friends and ride together. I said that Lesley had told me!"

"Did you call her 'Lesley' when you were interviewing her?"

"I thought you knew me better than that, Inspector, and trusted me. I will repeat. When Miss Porritt told me that Mrs Callender had referred to Lee's overfamiliarity with her as 'wandering hands', I asked her if Mrs Callender had had the same trouble with Lee, and she said, 'No'. I thought that was significant."

"Forget what I said. I wish I'd known all that before I saw Lee, but there was no way I could have delayed seeing him after I'd seen Woodman. I've scrubbed Kehoe. He was as sick as a dog when I produced the noose. I gave him an edited version of your interview with Leask, Blackwell, an' he was intrigued with what Leask didn't say, or what I didn't tell him that Leask said. Leask's timing was right, Kehoe's clock was fifteen minutes fast.

*****

Taylor had decided to take the tapes back to Kimpton, and gave Bennett and Blackwell the rest of the day off.

Blackwell said he would type up all his notes as a check, and Bennett decided to clear up in the kitchen.

Taylor, who had started to leave, came back.

"That's a good idea of yours, Blackwell, here's my notebook, you can do mine as well."

"That's a sauce, isn't it, Blackie?"

"Well, we weren't supposed to be doing any typing here; it would all be done at the station. I can cope."

He had finished by three, and after a cup of tea, Bennett drove them back to the cottage at Up Markham. Joan was pleased to see them and left them dozing in front of the fire while she went shopping.

After dinner, again beautifully cooked, but this time salmon, fresh salmon and salads followed by a crème caramel, which Blackwell praised as highly as he had done the lamb, Joan went to pay another visit to the expectant mother, leaving the two men to their pipes, their rum and talk. Bennett began the conversation.

"Do you think Buck's right about Lee being the killer. He's been pushing him very hard without taking him down to the station?"

"He's gone too far, I think. I've never seen Lee, but by all accounts, the murder required more than he seems to be capable of. I mean, that murder was planned carefully and cunningly. There was premeditation. True, he's got strength, and he's got a motive, if he is carrying on with Rose Callender, and he's the father of Dorothy's child to be.

"Take the ring, for example. Why should he draw attention to himself by tearing it off. The killer couldn't have been in a hurry. To me, taking the ring smacks of revenge, possibly not revenge, a gimmick, as they say in America.

"Who would think of taking the ring on that basis, Wiggy?"

"A woman?"

"Exactly, a woman, revenge a reason, jealousy another. If we knew what Rose Callender had against Dorothy I'd plump for her. She has an obvious link with Lee, and what if she wanted to get rid of the competition, or had some other good reason to hate her?"

"Would you go for Rosie?"

"I don't know, Wiggy. I can't really imagine someone like Rose Callender fighting over a little creep like Lee. But I am remembering what Lesley Porritt said about Rose having strong arms, and she had access to the stables, and she could know more about thuggee than she said."

"So you'd go for her?"

"If Lee turns out to be a dead end, yes I would."

*****

Wednesday, March 29th

After their nightly chat Blackwell had gone to sleep with the sound of driving rain on his bedroom window. He woke to the sound of his name being called and a hand shaking his shoulder.

"Blackie."

"What is it?"

"It's Woodman, from the stables, on the phone downstairs. He says he's found Lee hanging in the barn and he thinks he's dead."

Blackwell automatically looked at his watch; it was one-twenty on Wednesday morning. Blackwell tumbled out of bed.

"He sounds terrible, Blackie."

Blackwell shot down the stairs and picked up the phone.

"Mr Woodman, this is Detective Constable Blackwell, will you please tell me what has happened."

"I saw a light in the barn..." Woodman's voice was shaking,

"It was unusual at that time. I went down and put my boots on and went across. I went just inside the back door of the barn and..." his voice broke,

"I saw him hanging. I thought he was still alive until I realised that it was the draught from the door."

"Did you go right inside?"

"Only a few steps, I'd seen enough. You see, the light was on, that's what made me go over." His voice was breaking up again.

"What time was it when you saw him?"

"I got up at five past one to get a tablet. I know that was right because I looked at my clock. I saw the light because my bedroom window looks towards the barn. I suppose it was about ten minutes later when I called the sergeant, maybe a little more."

Blackwell looked at his watch, it was one twenty-five.

"I don't have to go in there again, do I Blackwell?"

"No, Mr Woodman. Go indoors but don't go to bed. Someone will come over to take a statement from you."

"Thank you. I think I'll have a little brandy."

"While you're dressing, Blackie, I'll phone Buck and tell him that we're both going to the barn."

Blackwell dressed quickly, and when he came downstairs Bennett told him that Taylor had seemed pleased. For one thing, only a doctor would be needed for a straightforward suicide. He would get hold of him and they would both come.

"We'll need some chalk, Wiggy, for the footprints, it's probably muddy as well as wet."

"I've got some and a tape measure. Lee probably came in the front so we'll go in the front so that we can mark Lee's as well as Woodman's prints." The rain had stopped but the forecourt of the barn was waterlogged and muddy.

The two men picked their way to the door and went in. Blackwell had not been inside before and was amazed by its size. The roof was almost hidden in darkness, the unshaded bulbs throwing what small light there was down on to the wooden floor.

Massive beams crossed and criss-crossed the roof space, joined at intervals by stout, wooden posts rising from the floor. On the far side, there were large bins which must, at one time, have held the tithes, but now held fodder. Along the opposite wall, where the back door was, bales of hay and straw were lined up. On the right-hand side a wooden partition divided the inner wall from the outer, resulting in the construction of Lee's room. As Blackwell went to close the door behind him he saw two large fixtures either side of it, and in the left-hand corner, close to the wall, a bin holding boxes. On the hook attached to the door a yellow anorak was hanging, and a cap. Both were soaking wet.

Lee's footprints, coming in, could clearly be seen, leading to the point where he was hanging. At that point there was one of the stout, wooden posts going up to meet the crossbeam, and it was to a cleat on the post that the rope had been fastened.

"Give me the chalk, Wiggy," he said to the sergeant who was standing looking up at the body.

"Take a look first, Blackie. We were wrong, it was Lee. See the ring on his little finger. I bet it was the one he tore off Dottie's finger."

"I hadn't credited him with remorse," Blackwell said, "but you never can tell."

"I'll chalk round the prints, Blackie."

Blackwell looked at the square wooden box which stood on the floor below Lee's feet. Away to the right was another similar box lying on its side. It was the classic scenario for suicide: Throw the rope over the cross beam, bring both ends down, tie one end in a noose and secure the other end round a cleat on the post, place your boxes one on top of the other, step up, put the rope noose round your neck, kick away the top box, and you were hanging ready to choke to death.

On an impulse, Blackwell felt the soles of the cowboy boots Lee was wearing. His hand came away wet and muddy. Bennett called him and he went round the post to find him.

"Here's where he got the boxes from. Look out for his prints, I'll chalk round these too." There were several boxes in the bin, all the same size. Blackwell said, "I just felt the soles of Lee's boots; they're still soaking and muddy. He can't have done it too long ago. The box he stood on should tell us." The two men went over to the box which lay on its side, the one Lee would have kicked away.

"It's on its side. If we had a longish piece of wood we could turn it over."

"Why bother with wood? I've got my thick gloves in the car. I'll get them. I'll tell you one thing, those boxes are heavy, and no wonder, they're reinforced inside, lined with metal. Why would that be?"

"They were used, no doubt, for sending heavy tack, stuff like stirrups, bits, spurs, all things that have to be protected. Were they marked?"

"I'll have a look." Bennett went to the corner. When he came back he said, "You were right, they were. A carrier's label addressed here. I looked at one that still had some of the stuff in it."

"They call it tack."

"I'll get my gloves."

With a glove each, and each taking hold of a corner. the box was turned on to the top on which Lee would have stood.

There wasn't a mark on it, only part of a cobweb. They turned the box on to each side but there were still no marks.

"That's odd," Bennett said

"It's not only odd, it's impossible." Blackwell thought for a minute.

"Let's have the tape measure, Wiggy, I've got an idea!"

Each side of the box was measured; all the sides were the same, the box was a perfect square.

"Are there any empty ones in that bin?"

"I'll have a look." Bennett went to the bin and returned lugging a box.

"Empty, the metal doesn't count, does it?"

"No. I'll give you a hand to put it on top of the one that's standing on the floor under Lee's feet."

They put it on top and stood back.

"It ought to reach his feet, oughtn't it Blackie?"

"And a bit further. When a person hangs, the rope is bound to stretch when it takes the strain of his body. By rights it should have reached down below the top of the box."

"What happened then?"

"What happened, Wiggy, was that Lee didn't hang himself, and he certainly didn't kick that box away. I think he was murdered, and I wouldn't mind betting he was killed in the same way as Dorothy Shervell, only this time, to make it look right, he was hanged afterwards to conceal the first mark, in the hope that it would be assumed that the rope noose had slipped. Then the scene was set to make it the perfect suicide, only like leaving the rope behind in Dorothy's case, he slipped up."

"What you're saying is that it was the same person who did both."

"It must have been: how else did the killer get the ring?"

"We'll have to tell Buck. He'll have a fit. I'd better tell him, I hope he'll take it better from me."

As the sergeant opened the front door to go out to his car another car drew up and Taylor got out.

"Were you waiting for me?"

"No, Buck, I was coming to phone you. We didn't expect you so soon."

"I didn't get much sleep; I was wondering whether Lee would break before this morning. He did, but not in the way I thought."

They were in the barn and Bennett turned to shut the door.

"Watch out for the chalk marks, Inspector, they were made by Lee when he came in."

"He must have had the rope with him, then."

"Shall I tell him or will you, Sergeant?"

"You tell him, Blackie, you're CID."

"Tell me what?" Taylor asked, looking from one to the other.

"Lee didn't hang himself, Inspector, he was murdered."

"You're not joking, are you? I can see that. Why is it murder?" Blackwell told him.

"We left the boxes where we put them. See for yourself, Inspector, and feel the soles of Lee's boots, then look on the box over there, no marks at all as there would have been had Lee stood on it."

Taylor went round checking. Straightening up he said, "So chummy did both, took the ring to set this up. He's certainly got more brains than Lee had. But he's still an amateur,"

"Or she," Blackwell said.

"That's what we must take into consideration now. The doctor should be here soon; I must go back and tell the old man, and alert the forensics."

"Could you find time to see Woodman? I did tell him you would want a statement, and I thought it ought to be you as you've seen him before."

"Quite right. I'll see him when I get back. Tell him that, no, I'll phone him from the car."

At the door Taylor turned.

"When this gets out, and it will, Billings seems to have a contact in the station, reporters will be flocking here. Stall them, Blackwell, if I haven't returned.

There's no need for both of you to stay, you can go to the church hall and get warm, Wiggy."

"I'd rather stay, Buck."

"Please yourself, I hope I shan't be long."

"What about dragging one of those bales of stuff against the wall, Blackie, it should be a bit warmer, and get us out of this draught?"

"Good idea."

They had just placed the bale when there was a knock on the front door. Blackwell opened it and the doctor came in rubbing his hands.

"At least it isn't in the open air this time, but it's still hellish cold in here. I would love to make an appearance where it's warm just once. That's him, is it? And I'm going to have to climb a ladder. Never mind, it looks like a nice, comfortable suicide."

"I'm sorry, Sir, but it isn't suicide. The Inspector agrees that it's murder."

"How did you come to that conclusion?"

"Just look at the boxes under his feet, Sir. The one that he's supposed to have kicked away is over there. Although the soles of his boots are still muddy there isn't a mark anywhere on it. And wouldn't you agree that if a man stood on a box, put the rope round his neck, and kicked the top box away, his feet should now be touching the box we put underneath as a test?"

"That's excellent detective work. You're Blackwell, aren't you? I met you at the other place. Did you sort it out?"

"The sergeant and I, Sir. We think he was killed in the same way as the girl and then hanged to make it look like suicide."

"And if his boots hadn't been muddy he would have got away with it. I will pay particular attention to his neck when I get up there, that is if you can produce a ladder."

"I'll get you one, Sir."

There was a long ladder lying alongside the fixture on the left of the front door and Bennett brought it and stood it up against the wooden post to which the rope was attached.

The doctor climbed slowly and cautiously up, enjoining Bennett to hold the bottom. The body was still swinging slowly as the result of the door opening and the doctor stopped the swing by grasping the rope between Lee's head and the cross beam. He looked closely at Lee's neck, and after touching Lee's face lightly, climbed down.

"It might have caused some concern in the P.M. there being two marks not quite together, but it is clear that he was taken from behind, as the girl was, and his thyroid cartilage crushed. Of course, that could happen with an amateur suicide."

"Could you give an estimate of the time of death, Sir? He was found by Mr Woodman, who owns the stables and rents the barn, at about five past one."

The doctor touched the soles of Lee's boots and looked at his finger.

"Still damp." He wiped his finger on his handkerchief.

"If he was dead at five past one, I would think he was probably killed at twelve-thirty or thereabouts. It's not so cold in here as it was the other morning. Certainly no later than twelve forty-five.

"I suppose the forensic team will turn up sometime, tell them to get cracking with the body. Goodbye."

Blackwell looked at his watch. It was three-fifteen and there was a knock on the outside door.

Bennett let Martin and two other men in, and the three of the forensic team went straight to the hanging figure.

"Who said a perfectly good suicide was murder?" Martin said, looking up at the body. "Who put the ladder up, or was it there when the body was found?"

"The sergeant and I said it was murder, the inspector agreed and so did the doctor who has been and gone. The ladder was put up so that he could have a good look at the body. By the way, the body is that of Joseph Lee who worked in the stables opposite. That's his room in there."

Blackwell pointed to the open door of the room in the corner.

"Well thank you very much, Blackwell, isn't it?"

"Yes. And Lee was probably killed in the same way as Dorothy Shervell, before being hanged."

"Do you think there's any need for us, lads," Martin said, meaning to be offensive, Blackwell was sure.

"Come on Wiggy," he said, let's go and sit over there where we won't be in the way."

They had just sat down on the straw bale when there was a tapping at the back door. Bennett, who had gone to open it, called to Blackwell, "It's Mrs Woodman with a life-saver."

Blackwell went to join them and took the tray with a Thermos and two cups on it while Bennett brought plates and some sandwiches.

Blackwell put the tray down on the straw and went to fetch another for Mrs Woodman to sit on.

"You will stay for a little while?"

"Yes, but please put the bale where I can sit with my back to that."

"Oh it's so cold in here, how can you stand it? Now I know what deathly cold means."

Bennett took off his coat and draped it round her shoulders.

"I haven't met you," she said to Blackwell, but I know who you are. I can't imagine why he would do it. I'm sure he didn't kill that girl. He was a proper baby if he was hurt, himself or animals. He loved horses."

"Did you ever go into the Shaw, Mrs Woodman?" Blackwell asked.

"It seems to have been an evil place in its day."

"And that reputation still persists. No, I have never even been over the bridge."

"Do you like it here; it seems such a small, enclosed place, as if everything is on top of one."

"You've obviously not lived in a village like this, Mr Blackwell. We find it ideal for our business, and civilisation is not all that far away, is it Sergeant?"

"I know what Blackwell means, Mrs Woodman. I felt that when I came back here after life in London. And you must admit that there is less than ever to do than there was a year ago."

"True. I can't argue with both of you." She laughed.

"Did you always live in a village?" Bennett asked.

"No, far from it. I was born, and lived, in Chester. My father kept horses and so I have always been connected with them."

"Did you get married there, then?" Blackwell asked.

"Yes. I met my husband because of horses. My father wanted someone to look after them and Stephen applied for the job. He had been at another stables in the city. Well, you know the rest."

"Thank you for the tea and sandwiches, Mrs Woodman. You've saved both our lives!"

"Thank you Sergeant, thank you Mr Blackwell. I see you've finished so I'll take the tray and say goodbye. Oh, the inspector did say that he would be coming to see Stephen when he gets back from Kimpton."

"How is he now, Mrs Woodman?" Blackwell asked

"Still very shaken, but he's much better than he was."

Expecting an invasion of reporters, Blackwell had bolted the front door after letting Martin and his crew in. There was a loud knocking on it and a voice called out: "It's Billings and a whole lot more reporters, we want to know what's going on."

"Big mouth," Bennett said.

"Wiggy, when I open the door close it immediately and bolt it. Don't open it until I knock three times."

Bennett opened the door only just enough for Blackwell to squeeze through. Billings stood in front of him.

"Just get back with the others, please."

"Who the hell do you think you are?"

"I am a police officer, Detective Constable Blackwell..."

"Where's Taylor?"

Blackwell looked round him.

"Do you want to hear what I have to say? If you do you'll have to wait until this gentleman," he hesitated over the word, "moves."

One of the reporters moved forward and took Billings by the arm, and said, "And who do you think you are, chum. Get back with the rest of us."

"Thank you. I am deputising for Inspector Taylor who has not yet returned from consulting the Chief Superintendent at Kimpton Police Station. There is a dead man inside the barn. Any further information will be given to you by Inspector Taylor when he returns. Thank you."

Bennett let him in and bolted the door again.

"Was that Billings?"

"Yes, one of the other reporters put him in his place."

"He wants a good kick up the..."

"Steady there, Sergeant," Martin said as he joined them.

"Everything checks out except the footprints going over to the bin in the corner. They're the same size as Lee's, but if he didn't make them, who did?"

"Probably the person who killed him had small feet too."

"That could be it. In which case it could have been a woman."

"Did you go in Lee's room?"

"Yes, and all we found was a load of porn magazines, a silver cigarette case with only his prints on it, and clothing. Could you face that lot out there again and call the ambulance crew in."

Blackwell went outside. Lights on top of a television van shone in his eyes. He could see the crew of the ambulance watching, and he put up his hand and beckoned them to come in. He waited while they brought the stretcher out and pushed their way through the reporters. Flashbulbs popped and the TV camera followed their progress. Bennett let them in and bolted the door. Blackwell and Bennett stood watching to see how the combined efforts of the forensic team and the ambulance crew would get Lee's body on to the stretcher.

One of the forensic team went right up the ladder while a second man stood on it halfway down. The man at the top held the rope between Lee's head and the cross beam and cut the rope, the man below taking the strain, as the body was suspended between them. Carefully, it was lowered until the two ambulancemen could guide it on to the stretcher and cover it with a blanket. The man at the top of the ladder cut the remaining rope from the beam, and Martin unwound the other end from the cleat and coiled the rope to take with them.

Blackwell went ahead outside when Bennett held the door open and told the reporters to stand back while the crew and the stretcher went through to the ambulance, running the gauntlet of the flashing cameras.

Martin paused and said to Blackwell:

"Don't worry, Doc will have his body in good time."

"Thank God that's over," Bennett said, after bolting the door again. "I wish I had my pipe, and where's Buck?"

"You called, Sergeant?"

Taylor had come quietly in the back way and walked over to join them.

"I've been over to see Woodman and got a statement from him. He looks alright now. How did it go with the reporters?"

"Billings played up but one of the others put him in his place."

"Mrs Woodman said she brought you tea and sandwiches."

"She saved our lives, Buck."

"I'd better get it over outside. I saw that the TV people were here this time. They're wasting their time. How did Martin take the news about Lee?"

"He said everything checked. The only snag was the second set of prints going over to the bin in the corner. He said they were the same size as Lee's but if he didn't make them who did. I said probably the person who killed him had small feet, he said maybe it was a woman."

"And possibly he was right. I'm going outside."

"I'll let you out, Buck,"

Taylor said no more to the reporters than he had done before when they had questioned him about Dorothy Shervell. What he did say was the same more or less, as Blackwell had said, and he referred them to Kimpton for further bulletins. They didn't like it this time either, but Taylor asked them to move off so that the villagers could go about their own lives without hindrance.

Once inside again, he told the other two that he had brought Parker and Norris back with him because it was essential that the barn should be guarded inside at all times. Parker and Norris were already at the church hall and would be sharing watch and watch about until Taylor was satisfied that the need to guard the barn was over.

"Did Martin's people check Lee's room?"

"Yes, and all they found was a load of porno and a silver cigarette case, and of course, clothing."

"Have you been in?"

"No, Inspector."

"Well, let's have a butcher's."

"There's a heater, Blackie, I wish we'd known."

"But is there a point out there?"

Taylor whistled. He was by the hanging wardrobe and had pulled the curtain,

"Look here, three suits, all nearly brand new, all tailored by the looks. He could never afford these on his money."

"And this is a silver cigarette case," Blackwell said, it's hall-marked."

"What about the chest of drawers?"

Bennett opened the top drawer. The other two came to stand beside him.

"Shirts, they look like silk, and pants and vests."

"They are silk. What about the next drawer?"

"Woollies, expensive looking, maybe camel hair," Bennett said.

"And the third drawer?"

"What he used to wear every day, and books. Jesus, look at the pictures, he must have had a mind like a cesspool."

Taylor had pulled a suitcase from under the bed.

"More porn, look at it, it's filth."

"I'll tell Woodman, he can burn them before his wife sees them if she should come in to clean up.

What was it Rose C. said, Blackwell? Woodman didn't like him. Possibly because Lee was bleeding him, but why?"

"What if Lee was pimping for Woodman," Bennett suggested.

"It's remote, with a nice lady like Mrs W. for a wife. But it makes you think."

"Isn't it more likely, Inspector, that he was getting money from Mrs Callender, if they were as close as we suspect?"

"He could have been getting it from both of them, but it does make Mrs C. a possible suspect for both murders, given the phoney footprint which just happened to be the same size as one of Lee's."

"What did Woodman have to add to what he told me earlier?"

"We'll deal with that when we get settled in at the church hall.

"See if there is a point, Wiggy, where the PCs could plug that heater in."

Bennett and Blackwell took either side of the barn to make a search, and it was Blackwell who found one in the skirting on the far side where the fodder was kept.

"That's fine. See if it works."

It did and, as it was near to the bales of straw as well, seemed an ideal place for someone to sit. And it was under one of the lights too.

"Buck, suppose we move one of those fixtures beside the front door across it so as to block it, the PCs will only have to watch one door, the back."

"That's a fine idea, Wiggy, I'll give you a hand."

"I'll do it, Inspector."

"Don't stop him, Blackie. It'll be lovely to see how he moves."

"Saucy bastard. To you, Wiggy."

"No, to you, Buck."

They were laughing so much they could hardly shift it, and Blackwell had to lend a hand.

"The time is now five o' clock. Is there still some food left at the hall?"

"Plenty. How did you get in, I've still got the key?"

"The Rev. lent us a spare. I'll get Norris or Parker, whoever wants to skip the first watch, to take it back. Will one of you stay here until I send one of them down?"

"I'll stay, Inspector. Woodman might come prowling around."

"Why do you want to keep him out, Buck?"

"I have my reasons, and I shall tell the PCs that on no account must they let anyone in. They are to say that no-one is allowed in until the investigation is over. If they persist, tell whoever it is to phone the hall. We'll go back there now, have a combined breakfast and dinner and get down to some talking."

*****

The meal was over and the three men had gone through all the evidence they had collected so far, and were as far away from a breakthrough as they had ever been.

"I want to see Kehoe again, and later on Mrs Callender. Blackwell, I want you to go and see Alice Shervell again. She may, or may not, help us by saying something important she may have left out when you saw her last time."

"Inspector, is it possible, do you think, that the village might be behind these murders as they were in the case of Jane Corby. I mean a Kangaroo Court?"

"Who would lead them, whose idea would it be?"

"Just an idea."

"Before I go, Wiggy, we haven't yet had time to do a house to house. Can you do it on your own?"

"Easily, and I'll take the spare key back to Cottew."

"Off you go, you two. We shouldn't be more than an hour so we'll be back before Norris has to relieve Parker at the barn."

Taylor didn't spend too much time with Kehoe who was really drunk this time, and accused Taylor of breaking up his friendship with Leask.

"I have a phone here, and I phoned the little bugger to find out what he said about me. I put the fear of God in him if he didn't tell me. He's a waspish little swine and he delighted in telling me what I was and what he'd told you which was one and the same thing. I told him never to come near me again, and do you know what he said, he said," and he poked Taylor with a finger, "he said, 'if I never see you again it'll be too soon.' So I said, 'Up yours,' that's what Shirley Maclaine said in *Sweet Charity*. Then I rang off. Now, get out, Taylor, before I throw you out."

Taylor was still laughing when he walked along to the end to wait for Blackwell, occupying his time by walking out on to the stretch of common land from where he could see French's Farm, part of the Shaw, and the stables in the foreground.

Blackwell, meanwhile, had shooed Lucifer away from the door and been greeted with pleasure by Alice Shervell. This time he was given the camomile tea, like it or not.

"I promised I would cast the cards for you, and I did so twice. That was enough. There is great joy coming for you but not before someone close to you has to suffer a tragedy. But it will all come right.

"It is terrible about the lad Lee."

"Do you think more than one person was involved, say, many people?"

"No, only one, and only one killed my daughter, but something links the two.

"One person?"

"Possibly, the cards were strange, first one, then another."

"Is there anything more you could tell me about Dorothy's friends who were Lee's too, anyone who would have a reason to kill?"

"There were a lot who wanted to, the cards told when I was casting them for her: she was surrounded by danger, as was Lee."

Blackwell had drunk half the tea, and so far as feeling settled in his stomach, felt slightly sick.

"The tea was fine, Mrs Shervell, and it was pleasant talking to you again. I must go now, but thank you for everything.

"Goodbye, Mr Blackwell."

The cards had told her that he would not call again, but she knew that the cards could be fickle.

Taylor and Blackwell walked slowly up Coopers Lane. The sky was overcast and it looked as if it might rain again. The entrance to Rabbit Shaw looked menacing, and it was hard for Blackwell to put out of his mind the horror which had been the dead girl.

He had a headache, and on an impulse, he said to Taylor:

"Would you mind, Inspector, if I went for a walk. I've not seen much of the village, and I thought I might go up the hill, over the stone bridge, along what they call the high meadows, and come down the path beside the Shaw back to the hall, that is, if you haven't anything special for me to do."

"Go ahead, Blackwell. You've done well, Wiggy too, finding out that Lee hadn't committed suicide was a plus, disappointing though it was as far as my theory of him as a murderer was concerned. Have a walk, I'll see you on your return."

As Blackwell walked along Mill Lane the sun came out, and he felt more cheerful when he crossed the bridge and began the ascent of the hill. 'Rabbit Shaw,' he had said to Bennett, 'I suppose it's a wood that had rabbits in it, but why its evil reputation?' Bennett had then told him something of its history as a one-time home to witches and satanists, and that in the clearing where Dorothy Shervell was found could still be seen the bottom half of the stone altar used by them for sacrifices. 'It's got this carving of a Penta-something still to be seen on it,' he had said.

As he climbed slowly there were hopfields on his left, and grazing land above the cottages in Mill Lane, on his right. The shepherd was there with his dog.

The hopfields ended and from then on to the top was scrub grass with patches of bush. It was almost behind one clump that he saw a girl sitting in a fold of the ground with her back to him. The manner in which her hair was tied back reminded him of Lesley Porritt. After their meeting on Tuesday he had come to the conclusion that he might well be falling in love with her. He walked across, his feet quiet in the grass, and saw that it was her. As he spoke she looked round, surprised.

"We meet again."

"How did you find me? I didn't think anyone knew my hidey-hole where I come to be alone, to sit and sketch."

"I'm sorry if I intruded."

"Are you being angry again? I didn't mean I wanted you to go."

"No, I'm not angry. Only I should have been disappointed if you had meant that."

He moved over to look at the sketch she was working on.

It was of the view across the fields and beyond to the outskirts of Kimpton with the spire of the old church in the background.

"I don't know much about art but I'd say this was pretty professional."

"Thank you. But I haven't really got the hang of perspective yet, my ayah taught me in India; she was a natural, like Grandma Moses in America. Perspective seemed to come naturally to her."

"May I sit down for a minute?"

"Of course; the grass is dry now. I heard the news about Lee from our paper boy. He must really have been in love with Dorothy, that's why he committed suicide, I suppose."

"The news certainly gets around."

"He said the village was full of reporters and the television people. How could we not be aware of it? We shall begin to wonder soon who's next."

"I don't think so, I think this will be the last."

"Are you near to solving Dorothy's murder then? People seemed to think Lee did it. That's why I said he must have been in love with her."

"I wish it was over."

"Why especially?"

"Because it's just possible that you might..."

"Please stop. Father's not at all well: Dr Calcott has given him tablets; it's his heart. He's worried because he sent the first two chapters of his book to a friend in London who is a Professor at the School of Oriental Studies and he hasn't heard a word yet."

"Is he hopeful? Are you?"

She looked away, plucking at her skirt.

"I don't know, I honestly don't know. He is, I'm sure. He's blind to everything except success which will take us back to London where he will be famous, and reunited with his old friends. So please don't bank on any more meetings other than the one today. I must be with him and help him." There were tears in her eyes.

"I've made you cry, and that was the last thing I wanted to do. It will be as you say, but you can't stop me hoping."

"No, I can't," she replied, as she dried her eyes.

"Why I came this way was because I wondered if I could cut across at the top and find a way down the other side, making it a circular tour."

"Yes, you can. At the top, turn right, there is a path, and follow it until it meets the other path going down. That's the way Young Tom would have come up to the high meadows, they are fields behind the path, to avoid going through the Shaw."

"Thanks. Goodbye Lesley, or is that forbidden," he said with a smile.

She laughed. "No, goodbye – David."

"You remembered. That's a start."

Following her directions, Blackwell found himself at the top of the hill on the other side, looking down at the rear entrance to the Shaw and part of the village. On his left was a stretch of meadow with cattle grazing and French's farm below. Behind the farm buildings the grass continued up to a tall wire fence, separating it from the dangerous area some one quarter mile square, pockmarked with dene holes, some of which, Bennett had said, were of unknown depths. It was on this ground that the Mill stream was born, turning into a fully-fledged river as it left Crowsett.

On his right was a field he had passed on his way up where sheep were grazing.

From his viewpoint, the village looked to be a perfect square, bounded as it was on the left by Coopers Lane and on the right by Hop Pole Lane. The most prominent features were the mill and oast, the church, and the old rectory.

The rear entrance to the Shaw was some fifteen yards away, and as he came nearer, he saw a young boy sitting on the base of a fallen tree. Nearer, he looked worried, with his head bent looking at the ground. It was clear that he hadn't heard Blackwell's approach.

"Hello." The boy looked up

"You look worried, can I help?"

He was a nice looking boy, about nine or ten years old, Blackwell thought, with fair curly hair.

"No-one can help me," the boy replied.

"Why is that? Perhaps I can help, I'm a detective, a police officer."

"I didn't see you down there on Monday. I saw Mr Bennett and some other policemen."

"I was away seeing someone. Look, here's my warrant card." The boy took it eagerly and Blackwell saw his lips moving as he read.

"This is your picture," the boy said, "and it does say you are a 'tec. But you haven't got a uniform."

"Detectives wear plain clothes."

"You're alright then, and I can tell you. I'm David too, David Farrar."

"You're Tom's brother..."

"Young Tom."

"Sorry, Young Tom."

"He found her," the boy said. "She looked awful, he said. He was sick twice. Will she be coming back?"

"Who, Dorothy?"

"Yes."

"No, David, she's dead; she can't come back."

"That's not what she said. I come up here to look for nests to rebuild so that the birds can find them again and not have to build new ones. I saw her on Sunday afternoon bending down by that big tree. Suddenly she turned round and saw me."

"What was she doing under the tree?"

"She was looking in a box. She put it back and then she saw me. I went to run but I slipped. When I got up she pinched my ear and she said that if I told anyone what I had seen she would haunt me, even if she was dead. I think she was in our bedroom last night, but I was afraid to tell Young Tom."

"She wasn't in your bedroom, David, and she can't haunt you, dead people can't, believe me."

"I feel better now."

"Good. Do you think you could find that box for me. It might be a clue which would help us to solve the murder."

"Yes David, it's under this big tree."

Kneeling down he dug with his hands and produced a square tin box. It had some colours left on it among the rust, and had probably held sweets or, most likely, biscuits at one time.

Blackwell opened it. On top was an expensive gold gate bracelet; his mother had one like it.

"That wasn't hers," the boy said, "it's mine. I found it. I should have given it to mum but I was afraid she would think I pinched it."

"When did you find it, and where, David?"

"Monday afternoon, after everyone had gone. I was looking for Old Whiskers, the water rat, he's got a hole in the stream bank. He wasn't there but this was."

"Which bank?"

"The one on the same side as the Shaw. It was dirty, so I cleaned it with my hanky and it's nice and shiny now."

A vital piece of evidence. The safety chain was broken, quite likely when whoever owned it was running out of the Shaw. Now he had to say to Taylor, 'It was dirty so he cleaned it with his hanky,' and wait for the explosion. He took his ball-point out of his pocket and poked underneath. There was a chamois pouch holding, no doubt, Mr Porritt's gold watch, a foolscap envelope stuffed with papers, items of costume jewellery, some good, others cheap, and at the bottom a red quarto notebook.

He shut the box and said to the boy, "This is an important clue, David, and I must take it to the Inspector.

"Would you like to come along?"

"Yes please, David"

Parker was in the main hall when the two entered, and Blackwell introduced David. Parker shook hands, and Blackwell said:

"He's found an important clue for us and it's only fair that he should give it to the Inspector"

"I'm sure the Inspector will be pleased, David," Parker said, and Blackwell and the boy went into the office.

Taylor had his mouth open and was about to speak when Blackwell pushed the other David forward.

"Hello Mr Bennett," he said

"Hello David, what brings you here?"

"David has something for the Inspector that he found in the Shaw, something of value. Inspector, this is David Farrar, brother to T-sorry Young Tom Farrar."

"Hello, Inspector,"

"Hello David," and he held his hand out which the boy shook.

David looked round at the other David.

"Now?" he asked.

"Now, David."

The boy took the box from Blackwell.

"Sir, I found this in the Shaw, and Mr David said it was an important clue and to give it to you."

Taylor took the box.

"Do you know what's in it, David?"

"Yes Sir, Dottie's pretties. Can I go now, David?"

"Yes, later on there will probably be a reward for you."

When the boy had gone Taylor set the box down on the desk and opened it.

"I take it you've already seen inside, Blackwell."

"Yes Sir."

Taylor had picked up his ball-point pen and was on the point of lifting out the bracelet when Blackwell said:

"Don't bother about the pen, Inspector. David found the bracelet in a hole in the stream bank, on the Shaw side, when he was looking for Old Whiskers, who is a water rat. He found it instead, on Monday afternoon when we'd all gone. It was all dirty so he cleaned it with his hanky until it was all shiny again."

"And you expect the little b- devil to get a reward?"

"There are other things which could be helpful, Inspector, but I have only seen what is near the top."

Taylor laid the bracelet on one side and took out the chamois bag, and from it the watch.

"Porritt's I have no doubt." Replacing the watch in the bag, he drew out the foolscap envelope and shook the contents out on to the desk. It consisted of £5 and £10 notes.

"Good Lord! Count it, Wiggy."

Next he took out the trinkets.

"Mostly cheap. There's only one thing left, Blackwell, and it had better be good. How much is there, Wiggy?"

"£250, Buck"

"Now where would she get that much money, from her clients?"

"I wouldn't think so, Buck, unless she's been saving up for ages."

"Perhaps this red notebook will enlighten us."

He opened the book and read out "Goats' milk sales? Where did they get goats' milk from?"

"I told you, Buck, French gave her a few goats. No doubt he processes her goats' milk with his own and she can sell hers. I do know some of the villagers have it, Rose Callender, for one."

"Well, she doesn't get much out of it, only £3 a week."

He leafed through the pages and was about to put it down when he turned three or four pages back.

"Jackpot, gentlemen. And your lad has his reward.

"A complete record of Dottie's blackmailing activities. What would you think of the initials: 'RC', 'ML' and 'EK'?"

"Rose Callender, Michael Leask and Edmund Kehoe," Blackwell said.

"Correct, and Wiggy, what about 'RW', 'KS' and 'GC'?"

"Roger Winch, Ken Sweet and George Coleman, three members of the darts team."

"Well, she wasn't greedy. £3 a month for everyone except Leask and Rosie, £5 for them. £19 a month from the blackmail, £12 from milk, £31, not a lot, but a regular income."

"In addition to what she got on her back."

"True. Let me have another look at the bracelet, I've got an idea."

Taylor felt in his pocket and brought out a small glass object, and almost screwed it into his left eye. He moved the bracelet slowly round, examining every part with the eyeglass. At one point he stopped and gave a grunt of satisfaction.

"It's alright, we're saved. This, he removed it from his eye, is an eyepiece, first cousin to a loupe, given to me, I might add, by a fence in the Met. It is a powerful little magnifying glass. Here, Wiggy, see if you can find a tiny scratch mark on one of the divisions. I warn you, it is tiny."

After inspecting it, Bennett gave it to Taylor.

"I can't see a thing, Buck."

"You try, Blackwell."

Blackwell carried out the same scrupulous examination, going back over a section twice. At last he looked up.

"I saw it, it looked like an 'x'."

"It did, but I don't think it is. I think it's two initials back to back. It's not a perfect 'x', and I think the first initial is 'F' backwards and the second 'C' as it is: 'FC'. This is the mark a working jeweller would inscribe on a piece if he repaired it, or when he made it. Find 'FC' and we find out who brought it in for repair.

"Blackwell, take this into Kimpton and ask to see Mr Gibbon at James Walker. If he says it's his mark tell him you want to know, in confidence, who had it repaired and that you're acting for me. If there's any query he can phone me here.

"One very important bit of information from the house to house. Tom Farrar, the father, was coming from a late stint at the mill and saw a woman run across the road from the barn and go in the front gate of the White House. He couldn't identify her, but it was a woman, and he does remember the time because he was so late. It was twelve-twenty, and there was a light in the barn.

"It must have been Mrs Callender, and this ring business, I thought that could have been the work of a woman. It all seems to be coming together. I hope so, any way I'm going to see her this afternoon, but you get going for Kimpton."

Rose Callender was wearing a tailored blue suit, which went with her colouring, when she opened the door to Taylor.

"Now I've had all three," she said, "the sergeant, the young detective, and the inspector. Finally, I hope. Do come in please."

Her perfume was a bit overpowering, but she was certainly an attractive woman. He didn't mince his words once they were seated.

"Why was Dorothy Shervell blackmailing you, Mrs Callender?"

She laughed. "You're joking, of course, Inspector."

"It's no joke, I'm very serious, I assure you. You see, Dorothy left a record of the people she blackmailed for one reason or another. £5 a month in your case, am I right?"

She looked stunned and it was a moment before she replied.

"Alright, she was. Even dead she spreads her evil. It was right for her to die."

"Isn't that rather sweeping, Mrs Callender?"

"Not sweeping enough, Inspector. I am sure you know the reason why."

"You rather gave yourself away when my DC was interviewing you when you referred to Lee as Joseph. You were the only one who did that. He was in your car, wasn't he?"

"Yes, yes. I am a comparatively young woman, and no different from others who lose husbands and find themselves seeking love, or what passes for love these days. Stephen Woodman was a candidate, but I repulsed him. Not only did I basically dislike him, but Tessa, his wife, is my friend. Joseph, coarse both in speech and manners, but an accomplished lover, provided, or rather satisfied my need, and his demands were reasonable. That is until the girl was killed, when he thought he would take over. I had given him money and I was not prepared to give him any more. I told him that on Sunday night. He couldn't have killed Dorothy because he was here with me until well after midnight on Monday morning."

"That brings me to this morning, Mrs Callender. You were seen running from the barn and entering your front gate at about the time Lee was murdered"

"Murdered! But I thought he committed suicide."

"That is what we want people to think, and the information is confidential. I have told you because that's how important it is for me to know the movements of everyone who knew Dorothy and Lee."

"The murders were connected then."

"They were."

"I understand now what you want from me.

I was not running from the barn, but from outside the barn. Let me explain. Last night, just before midnight, if you want the exact time I'm not sure because I was watching television when Joseph came in the back way. I explained to Mr Blackwell that I record and watch later on, Asian movies. I have a clock on top of the TV, as you see, but I was so surprised that I did not look before I switched off. He had been drinking, too much, which was unusual for him, and he was frightened, more than frightened, frantic. He said he had to get away, you were going to frame, is that right, frame him?"

"Yes."

"Frame him for Dorothy's murder. I had made him promise that he would not reveal details of our relationship, and in that respect, he was honourable. He wanted money, I refused, I said I had given him enough. After arguing some more he left, saying as he went, 'If you won't, I know who will.'

"I watched him go over to the barn and I saw the light come on, I thought maybe I should help him, so I went out with my handbag and crossed over but changed my mind and came back. I thought if I gave way it could start up again as before."

"Some times, please, Mrs Callender. You say you don't know what time it was when he first came in, can you guess?"

"Yes I can. The video recorder I have, and I suppose most others, has numbers showing when a programme stops. I calculated how much I would have to make up, in time, before the film finished, and I would say that when he came in it was not less or more than ten to twelve. When he left I did look at the clock, it was a quarter past twelve. And when I came back after crossing the road, it was twelve-seventeen exactly. As you see, my clock has a second hand and a minute hand which sweeps round."

"Do you notice time as accurately as that?"

"Inspector, I was in charge of my husband's polo ponies in India. Mounts have to be changed, not haphazardly as some do, but to a strict time schedule as Charles insisted on. He loved his ponies, and so did I."

"Thank you very much, Mrs Callender. You have been most helpful, and courteous, more helpful than you'll ever know."

"Goodbye, Inspector. I have seen not only three policemen, but three gentlemen."

Blackwell hadn't returned when Taylor joined Bennett in the church hall.

"How did it go, Buck?"

"Perfect. All I want now is a positive ID for the bracelet and we'll be home and dry. I hope Blackwell gets back soon with his dope. When he does I can visit Woodman and check the statement he made this morning which was not all that helpful."

Blackwell came into the office as Taylor finished speaking.

"Success?"

"Yes Inspector, Gibbon was very helpful; he didn't repair it or sell it but he knew who probably did by the mark on the bracelet. It was a fellow who used to work for him, François Cloutier, who now has a business in Stone Street in Yarborough. I went there..."

"And?" Both Taylor and Bennett were hanging on his words.

"Not only did he repair the bracelet a fortnight ago, but he sold it two years ago. He did a repair job quickly because it was needed urgently, but he said that it could go again if she wasn't careful..."

"I'll thump you, Blackwell."

"The big finish, gentlemen, is that the lady was Mrs T. Woodman..."

"I knew it," Taylor said

"There's more, Inspector. It was sold two years ago to a Mr Woodman, and I have the slip showing that he paid by credit card. Cloutier remembers him."

"You knew it all the time, Buck," Bennett said in amazement.

"No, Wiggy, only this afternoon for certain. Rose Callender told me the truth. She couldn't have killed Lee because he was with her until about the time he was murdered, and he couldn't have killed Dottie because he was with her until well after the deadline.

"And she didn't come from the barn when Tom Farrar saw her, she came from outside the barn. Lee had asked for money, she refused, he was frantic, said I was going to frame him for Dottie's murder. He kept quiet about where he was, and lied, because he had promised not to implicate her.

"She started to change her mind when he went back to the barn and she went across, changed her mind again and went back to the house. The time he entered the barn and put the light on was twelve-fifteen, and she saw it was still on at twelve-thirty. Tom Farrar also saw it on at twelve-fifteen"

"So the Woodmans are heavily involved."

"Up to their armpits, Blackwell. I'm certain the murders were a joint operation, she probably killed Dottie, and he certainly killed Lee. I'm going round there now; I want to put a little pressure on and wait, hopefully for the pop. He put the bracelet in his pocket with his notebook."

"Buck, before you go, why did you suspect Woodman in the first place?"

"There were the lies he told, but more than that, it was the second set of footprints leading to the bin where the boxes were. Small feet, like Lee's, whose were they, Martin said. The first time I met Woodman I looked at his feet, that was a habit of mine in the Met, to see if a kick was on the way, and Woodman's feet were no bigger then Lee's."

"It's cold again, Inspector," Mrs Woodman said when she opened the door, "come into the study where it's warm. Stephen is in there already. You won't need me, will you?"

"If you can spare the time, Mrs Woodman, then I can check both your statements."

"Here he is, Stephen."

"Tessa saw you coming. Sit down, Inspector. Did I hear the word 'statement'."

"Yes Sir. You were a bit shaky this morning…"

"That's putting it mildly. Sit down, Inspector, ah, I see. He's waiting for you, Tessa." Taylor took out his notebook.

"Can I go back to Sunday night first, now that we have another incident. When you both came back from Yarborough, Mrs Woodman went straight indoors because she had a headache, is that right?"

"Yes, I get them from time to time."

"Your inability to find Lee, Mr Woodman, meant you had to do 'stables', I think you call it, on your own. He told you the next morning that he had seen you coming and had gone off to keep a date."

"Quite right, Inspector."

"That was a lie. He told me he went to Kimpton after you left and went to the cinema but I think that was a lie too.

"Now, last night and early this morning. You woke up at a quarter to twelve, Mr Woodman, and went over to your dressing table for a tablet. Your windows overlook the barn and you saw that there was no light in there."

"Correct."

"You woke up again this morning at twelve-twenty and looked out of the window while you were taking another tablet, and there was still no light."

"Correct again."

"When you got up a third time, still suffering, at five past one, there was a light, causing you to go downstairs and go over to the barn because a light on at that time was unusual."

"That's right, Inspector."

"On your way downstairs Mrs Woodman heard you and called out."

"And he told me not to worry."

"With your coat and boots on you only went a few steps into the barn where you saw Lee hanging."

"A horrible sight, I was shaking when I came back to the house."

"And telephoned to Sergeant Bennett and spoke to my DC, Blackwell. By now, Mrs Woodman, you had come downstairs to see what the trouble was."

"An excellent summary, Inspector."

Taylor felt in his pocket and produced the bracelet, laying it on the desk. We've had a bit of luck. David Farrar found this on Monday afternoon when he was looking for a water rat in the bank of the stream just outside the Shaw. It was dirty, he said, so he cleaned it with his hanky until it was shiny again."

"That's terrible, Inspector, he wiped the fingerprints off," Woodman said.

"I'm afraid so. Would you have any idea, Mrs Woodman, who would own it, it looks expensive?"

"It is expensive, too expensive for me. What do you think, Stephen?"

Woodman took the bracelet and examined it.

"Well, it's not Tessa's, I can vouch for that, because if it had been I would have bought it, and I certainly did not. I can tell you who might own one like this, Rose Callender. Eh Tessa?"

"She certainly wears a lot of jewellery, but this is a clue, isn't it Inspector?"

"It's the only one we have. I must check with her. If you want to go, Mrs Woodman, you can."

"Thank you. I'll get on with our dinner for tonight."

Both men rose as she left.

"Now that she's gone, Sir, I can tell you that Lee did not commit suicide, he was murdered."

"Good God! Who could have done it, you don't think..."

"I am not naming anyone at present."

"But, Inspector. If Lee came in prepared to hang himself, instead of going to his room, and went straight to the place where I saw him hanging, how can it be murder?"

"A good point, Mr Woodman, but I can assure you that it was. For the time being I should be glad if you would keep it to yourself."

"I will. I don't envy you, Inspector, now you have two murders on your plate."

"I realise that only too well, Sir. You and Mrs Woodman have been very helpful and very patient. Good night, and thank Mrs Woodman for me."

"I'll see you out, Inspector." At the door they shook hands and Taylor whistled a little tune as he made his way back to the church hall.

Taylor stopped to talk to Norris.

"Go down to the barn and bring Parker back with you. Tell him to bolt the door at the back and see if he can turn the key in the lock of the front door as you leave. There's an oilcan in my car; take it with you. We've finished with the barn, and switch the lights off."

"You are seeing a happy man," Taylor said, as he sat down in the office. "They fell right in the manure. Mrs W. didn't go near the Shaw when they returned from Yarborough, the bracelet wasn't hers, Woodman confirmed it as well, and he stuck to his story that there was no light in the barn at twelve-twenty when we know Lee was back in the barn at twelve-fifteen, according to Mrs Callender, and Tom Farrar. Finally, when I told Woodman that Lee was murdered he said, 'if Lee came in prepared to hang himself instead of going to his room, and went straight to the place where I saw him,' note that, where he saw him hanging, having said twice that he only went a few steps into the barn when he found Lee hanging, 'how could it be murder?'. But he couldn't know that Lee went straight to the point where he was hanged, unless he'd been there himself. But he hasn't been allowed near the barn. Could Mrs Woodman have seen them when she brought your stuff in? Did she go over near the other door?"

"No. She insisted on sitting with her back to Lee, and we were over near the back door to be out of the way of the forensic people. But how did he get Lee to come straight to the place where he wanted him?"

"I wondered that too, Buck."

"He must have put something there to attract Lee's attention as soon as he came in, maybe the boxes."

"Or the rope, already hanging."

"That's good, Blackwell. He had the rope all ready to hang him.

I think it went like this: Woodman comes to the barn in advance with boots on, carrying his sock-slippers I saw him wearing the first time I met him. He makes the few steps into the barn with his boots, changes them for the slipper things, and carrying the boots, goes over to hang the rope and hide behind that large fixture. Lee comes in, takes his coat and hat off, turns round and sees the rope and wonders what the hell has happened. Woodman is behind him and takes him with the garrotte, hangs him first, then changes to his boots, collects the boxes and arranges them under Lee's feet, pushes the top one away, to make it look as if Lee had kicked it away, changes back into his slipper things, which he could probably put in his coat pocket, and goes out carrying his boots. Goes back indoors and waits until a reasonable time elapses, then phones."

"That's masterly, Buck.

"Masterly, Wiggy, I'm overwhelmed. But it has proved one thing: we are a team, and that includes Parker and Norris. What I want now is the real motive for killing both Dottie and Lee. I'd like to know that, and whether Mrs W. was wearing that bracelet when they were with the Forrests at Yarborough on Sunday night, but she must have done, and anyway, I have enough to ask for warrants for both of them because I'm certain they were in it together."

"Mrs C. had the strength, Lee had it, but did Mrs Woodman have it?"

"Nice point, Wiggy, and Woodman would have it too, but don't forget Mrs Woodman was into the mating business as well, that needed some strength."

"Just a suggestion, Inspector, but when Mrs Woodman was talking to us she said she was born and lived in Chester where she met and married her husband."

"That does give me an idea," Taylor picked up the phone and asked for and was given the number for the Chester Police Station. He dialled and asked for the CID office and was put through.

"DI Taylor, Kimpton Police, who am I speaking to?"

"Buck, Buck Taylor. DCI Inkpen."

"Inky, you a DCI, I bet you had to grovel."

"Saucy. I was lucky, Buck. You still a DI then?"

"Yes. Look, Inky, would you know anything about a chap named Woodman who lived on your patch?"

"Stephen Woodman, yes. He was ex-Army, a P.T.I., I believe, married into money, his boss's daughter. Why?"

"He's living here with his wife. Here is a little village called Crowsett, in Midshire. Anything special you can tell me?"

"The only thing I remember was that they were both into martial arts. He ran a course at the local adult centre, she helped him."

"Thanks a lot, Inky. Nice talking to you."

"And you, cheers Buck."

"That's the missing piece, or one of them. The Woodmans were into martial arts, Woodman used to run a class there. I'll feel better when I apply for warrants in the morning. I'll want you with me, Wiggy, when we pay them a visit. I'll give them time to eat breakfast and do whatever they have to do with the horses, and then we'll step in. Blackwell, you'll be needed at the station bright and early to set up an incident room, and later on, to be available in the charge room. Wiggy, you'll be in the other incident room with the Woodmans. I'll take Parker and Norris back with me and see you in the morning, Wiggy."

"Could I come as well, Inspector? I shan't be needed here again."

"You're welcome to stay another night with us, Blackie."

"Thanks Sergeant, but I do have stuff waiting for me. Some other time for sure. Can I pick up the stuff I left at your place tomorrow?"

"Any time, Blackie. It's been a pleasure to have you. Joan thinks so too."

*****

Thursday, March 30th

At ten o'clock Taylor and Bennett were knocking on the door of the stables. Again it was Mrs Woodman who opened the door.

"Good morning, both of you this time. Stephen's out in the yard."

"Would you fetch him please, and would you tell him that it's urgent."

"You sound serious, Inspector; has anything else happened?"

"It is serious, Mrs Woodman, and we would like to see both of you inside."

Her face changed. "Of course, you'd better come into the study."

Woodman, followed by his wife, came in. "What the devil do you mean by frightening the life out of my wife? What is it that's so urgent?"

"Both of you sit down please."

They did so.

Taylor stood. "Tessa Woodman, I hold a warrant for your arrest on suspicion..."

Woodman was on his feet. "Have you gone mad, Inspector?"

"Sit down, Mr Woodman."

"You dare to tell me that in my own house."

"Yes Sir. I am a police officer, and I hold warrants for the arrest of both of you. Please listen. If you wish to say anything you may do so when I have finished serving the warrants." Woodman made no reply.

"Tessa Woodman, I hold a warrant for your arrest on suspicion of the murder of Dorothy Shervell in the wood known as Rabbit Shaw, in the village of Crowsett, in the County of Midshire, on the night of Sunday, March 26th, 1995. Another charge may follow.

"You are not obliged to say anything, but anything you do say in answer to the charge will be taken down and may be used in any trial that could follow. Do you understand, and do you wish to say anything?"

"Say nothing, Tessa, he's bluffing."

"Mrs Woodman?"

"I have nothing to say."

"Stephen Maurice Woodman, I hold a warrant for your arrest on suspicion of the murder of Joseph Lee in the tithe barn in the village of Crowsett, in the county of Midshire, on the morning of Wednesday, March 29th, 1995. Another charge may follow. You are not obliged to say anything, but anything you do say in answer to the charge will be taken down and may be used in any trial which may follow. Do you understand the charge, and do you wish to say anything?"

"Go to hell!"

"And that is all you wish to say?"

Woodman didn't reply.

"The time is now ten twenty-five, is that right sergeant?"

"Yes Sir."

"Mr and Mrs Woodman, I am taking you to Kimpton Police Station where I shall question you further, and you may make statements before you are formally charged."

"Inspector."

"Yes, Mrs Woodman."

"Why are you doing this to us?"

"I do not have to answer that, Mrs Woodman, but I will. It is because I am not satisfied with the statements you and your husband made on Monday, and last night."

"Do we need to take anything with us, and what about the horses?"

"At present you need take nothing with you. The Chief Inspector is arranging for you to appear before the court for a preliminary hearing this afternoon. If there is a case to answer, you will be remanded in custody until your trial at Yarborough Crown Court. That is the usual procedure. Can you get someone, Mrs Callender for example, to help with the horses?"

"Yes, I think she would, Stephen, and Lesley too. May I telephone?"

"Of course."

"I'll use the one in the hall."

"And may I go upstairs please teacher and change my clothes?"

"I'd like the sergeant to go with you."

"Is that necessary, Inspector?" asked Tessa Woodman who had finished her telephone call to Rose Callender.

"Just a precaution, Mrs Woodman."

"Rose Callender is coming to see me, is that alright?"

"Quite alright. You may prefer to see her in another room."

"Thank you, I do."

The doorbell rang.

"That will be Rose. May I answer it?"

"Of course."

Taylor heard the two women greet each other, and it sounded as if Tessa Woodman was close to tears. There was a long conversation in another room before he heard the front door close.

Woodman came down the stairs followed by Bennett.

"Rose has agreed to look after the horses, Stephen, she's out there now."

"Mr Woodman, you are allowed to have a solicitor present when you are interviewed. Would you like to telephone now?"

"Yes, I'll phone Kennard, Tessa. When will we need him?"

"If we can leave soon, say eleven-fifteen."

Woodman phoned from the study and spoke.

"He'll be there," he said.

"We can go now, if you're both ready."

"I'll just get my coat," Tessa Woodman said. "I've given Rose a spare key."

*****

One of the incident rooms at Kimpton Police Station had been prepared. In addition to a tape recorder, a WPC was ready to take shorthand notes. Blackwell had earlier telephoned Cloutier, the jeweller, and he had seen the Woodmans arrive without being visible himself. With the credit card slip in his possession, Taylor had seen no need for a line-up. Cloutier had, at Blackwell's request, described Mrs Woodman, and repeated his meeting with both Woodmans.

On his way down in the car, Woodman had asked about bail. Taylor had made it clear that bail was not usually granted for a capital crime. He had said nothing about the possibility of bail for his wife, but he intended to tell Kennard that if he asked for bail for Mrs Woodman, the police would not oppose the request. He was sorry for her, and planned to see her first, on her own, because he thought that if either of them broke it would be her.

Kennard had arrived and the two had talked, Kennard agreeing on the matter of bail. He outlined to Kennard the pattern the interviews would take, and confirmed that he would be prepared to break off an interview if Kennard and he considered it necessary, thinking rather of Mrs Woodman than her husband.

WPC Lucy Ford was ready at the door of the incident room to fetch the Woodmans in, Mrs Woodman first. Blackwell was waiting in the charge room, and Sergeant Bennett was looking after the Woodmans in a second incident room.

Taylor switched on the tape recorder and set the scene, noting the time and the people present.

"OK Lucy, wheel Mrs Woodman in. Only Mrs Woodman, if her husband cuts up the sergeant can deal with him"

Taylor laid the bracelet on the table beside his notebook. Mrs Woodman came in and Taylor asked her to sit opposite him within easy reach of the desk microphone which stood between them.

He explained the procedure to be followed, including the preparation of a statement which she could read and sign, if she chose to make one. He asked her if she understood and she said that she did. "Mr Kennard is here to help you if you need him. Do not hesitate to consult him if you feel you need to."

He switched on the tape recorder and gave details of the interview to take place.

Taylor repeated the caution he had given earlier and said:

"Do you now wish to make a statement, Mrs Woodman?"

She looked haggard, and Taylor had noticed her eyeing the bracelet.

"You know, don't you? It was the bracelet, wasn't it?"

"Tessa," Kennard called out.

"No, Harry, I want to tell it, all of it. That's what you want, isn't it Inspector? I must tell it, don't you see?"

"Go on, Mrs Woodman."

"Tessa, I beg you!"

"It's alright, Harry, I know what I'm doing. Yes, Inspector, I did kill that girl. May I tell it from the start?"

"Please do, Mrs Woodman. Are you sure you're alright?"

"Perfectly, now. Will you first tell me how you knew the bracelet was mine when all the dirt had been rubbed off, and the fingerprints?"

"When jewellers repair an article most leave their mark on it. Mr Cloutier did, a tiny mark, his initials."

"And you were clever enough to find it and trace him all the way to Yarborough?"

"I'll begin." Taylor saw that she was more composed.

"It was on Saturday morning, last Saturday. I was in the High Street shopping and Dorothy Shervell stopped me. 'We should talk,' she said, so I walked along with her. 'I am carrying your husband's child,' she said. I told her I didn't believe her. Then she gave me details. She said all the men she went with wore some protection, she insisted on it because she had been told that the pill might be dangerous for a condition of her blood or something. I didn't know that Stephen was one of her clients. She said he refused to wear anything, 'It didn't feel the same,' he said. As he paid well, she agreed. She did take the pill at first but it made her ill so she stopped.

"I said it was a load of rubbish, but she convinced me, giving me explicit details that only anyone who had seen him naked would know. She detailed the two scars and the rough way he made love. It was true; it was because of his roughness that I had given up sleeping with him long ago. As you know, we had separate rooms. Of course I knew that he had girls, Lee got them for him, and when he said he was going to the barn I knew what for. She wanted money for an abortion, a lot of money, £500 to start with. We didn't keep that amount of money, I said, but she replied that Joe had told her we had a reserve that never went to the bank or was never taxed. I said that I must consult Stephen. 'Make it fast,' she said 'I want it tonight.'"

"Would you like some water, Mrs Woodman?"

"Yes please."

When the water was brought, Mrs Woodman took a long drink and continued. "You can guess that Stephen denied everything she had said until I told him the personal details she had told me. Then he broke down and cried. I was not impressed; he had cried before when he was in a jam. He stopped, and then he said that we had to kill her and Lee who was bleeding him as well. If we didn't we'd be out of business if we gave them money, or if we didn't. I love the business, the horses, so like a fool, I agreed. I had to tell her that it would be Sunday night because we would be out on Saturday night, and until about eleven on Sunday night. She would be bound to choose the Shaw for the hand-over so as we met I would be holding what looked like a packet of money. I would start to hold it out but draw her attention to something behind her. When she turned I was to garrotte her with the piece of rope Stephen would give me. Then I had to take the ring off her finger because he would need it for when he killed Lee, and had to not forget to bring the rope back.

"It all went according to plan except that Dorothy tried to turn back when she felt the rope but she caught her heel which stopped her, and I did it. I tore the ring off, but I was panicky, and I didn't think she was dead so I tied the rope tightly and left it. I had gloves on."

She sat back exhausted.

"Only one more question for now, Mrs Woodman. What shoes did you wear?"

"My slipper-socks, Stephen and I both have a pair, you saw them. Can I lie down now please, I don't feel very well."

"Of course. Lucy, take Mrs Woodman to your rest room and get some tea. I may have to see you again, but only for a little while, Mrs Woodman."

"You were lucky, Frank. But how could a decent woman like that have done it."

"Like she said, Harry, she loved horses." The telephone rang and Taylor picked it up.

"Taylor."

There was a smile on his face when he put the phone down.

"That was Bloxham. The court for this afternoon is two-thirty."

"Will you tell them or shall I?"

"You, Harry."

He had switched off the recorder when he had spoken to Bloxham and he switched it on again to set the scene for Woodman.

After handing Mrs Woodman over to another WPC, Lucy had returned, and Taylor asked her to bring Woodman in.

Woodman's opening remark after he had sat down was predictable.

"Where's my wife? Why weren't we seen together. Why didn't you insist, Harry?"

"I will answer that, Mr Woodman," Taylor said, "it was because you were charged separately, each with a different crime.

"I will tell you exactly what I told your wife. This interview is being recorded, and shorthand notes are being taken. If you choose to make a statement, that statement will be typed and presented for your signature.

"Now I will repeat the caution I administered to you and your wife at your house, The Stables, in the village of Crowsett, this morning. Do you understand what I have said?"

Woodman did not reply. Taylor went ahead and administered the caution. "Do you now wish to make a statement in answer to the charge of murder which I read to you this morning, and which I have repeated here?"

"Don't bother. It's a load of rubbish as I told you before, and you haven't a shred of evidence to substantiate it. I don't have to say anything, do I Harry?"

"No, Stephen."

"You say I have no evidence, Mr Woodman, but let me present a few items. One: you said that when you returned from Yarborough on Sunday night your wife went straight indoors because she had a headache. That was a lie, wasn't it? Your wife, with your approval, went up to Rabbit Shaw where she killed Dorothy Shervell, bringing back the ring, which you needed, but leaving the rope behind."

"If she said so, Harry, she's lying. She's been funny lately, I think it's what they call the change, she'd say anything."

"That's not so, Mr Woodman. She told me of one piece of evidence which was not made public and which could only have been known to someone who was present in the Shaw.

"Two: you said on two occasions that there was no light in the barn at twelve-twenty. In fact, we have two witnesses who saw the light at that time, and also at twelve-thirty. Your clock, you said, was a quartz clock and was never wrong."

"It probably was wrong."

"No. Mr Woodman. After we left I had the clock tested and it was accurate to a second."

Woodman, like Lee before him, was starting to sweat, Taylor noticed.

"Three: You told me, and confirmed it twice, that when you went over to the barn and found Lee hanging you did not go right in. The prints made by your boots confirm this. And yet, when I told you that Lee had been murdered, you said, and I quote: 'It must have been suicide; why else did he come straight to the point where he hanged himself instead of going to his room?'"

"What of it, I saw his footprints?"

"How did you see them, Mr Woodman? Those footprints were made on the opposite side of the barn to where you stood, on the floor. You haven't been inside the barn since. The police did not release any information about them, and neither did the three people who are conducting the investigation, Sergeant Bennett, Detective Constable Blackwell, and myself. I suggest that you could only have known about the prints if you had been in the barn when Lee entered, and I think you killed him first and then hanged him to make it look like suicide.

"Where were you hiding, behind the fixture next to the door? And what lure did you put out to draw Lee to the point where you killed him, the rope already hanging, or perhaps, the boxes?"

Woodman said nothing at first and then suddenly exploded.

"Perhaps I did go right in; I was shocked, you know that. But what about the bracelet? It wasn't Tessa's. I said it might belong to Rose Callender; did you go and see her?"

"I have done, Mr Woodman. Lee was with her before he came back to the barn at twelve-fifteen. She saw the light go on. Tom Farrar also saw the light on at that time. Yet you said yourself there was no light on at that time. The bracelet? You bought it for your wife two years ago from Cloutier, the jeweller in Stone Street, Yarborough, and your wife had him repair it a fortnight ago. I have the slip showing that you paid for it with your credit card.

"Finally, if your wife did not murder Dorothy Shervell, and you did not murder her, how is it that the ring which was torn off the girl's finger appeared on the little finger of Lee's hand? I suggest to you that you put it there after you killed him."

"How could I have killed him? My boots were muddy, why didn't my footprints show up?"

"Could I suggest to you that you were wearing your slipper-socks, like your wife was?"

"Don't say any more, Stephen," Kennard said.

"Listen to him, Mr Woodman."

"I will say one thing more, Harry. Inspector, the newspapers said the murders were similar to those carried out by Thugs. How would we know how to kill like that?" he added, smiling at Kennard.

"Do you remember a Detective Chief Inspector in Chester named Inkpen, Mr Woodman? He remembers you running a class in martial arts at the local adult education centre; your wife was a member of the class."

"You won't say anymore, will you Stephen?" Kennard asked, and Woodman shook his head.

"The procedure now, Mr Woodman, is that you are formally charged. I said that another charge might follow and I now have enough evidence to charge you with conspiracy to murder Dorothy Shervell in the local wood known as Rabbit Shaw in the village of Crowsett, in the county of Midshire, on the night of Sunday, March 26th. You are not obliged to say anything in reply to the charge but anything you do say will be taken down and may be used as evidence in any trial which may follow."

"No comment."

"Do you understand what I have said, and is that your answer?"

"Yes, damn you!"

"Lucy, call Sergeant Bennett, will you.

"Stephen Maurice Woodman, you will now be taken to the charge room where you will be formally charged with murder, and conspiracy to murder, as specified.

"After being charged you will be remanded in custody to appear before a court at two-thirty this afternoon. If it is decided by the court that there is a case to answer, you will be further remanded in custody until the next sitting of the Crown Court at Yarborough. Do you understand what I have said?"

"Yes. Will you be at the court, Harry."

"Yes I will."

Sergeant Bennett took his arm, Woodman shook it off.

"I can walk, I don't need your help."

Taylor switched off the recorder and took out the tape, putting a fresh one in.

"Did you get it all down, Moira?"

"Yes, Inspector."

"Nip off then and type it up; Mrs Woodman's statement first, four copies altogether, bring her statement in when you've finished it. Lucy, see if Mrs Woodman is up to taking a little more."

Mrs Woodman looked pale but composed. Taylor switched the recorder on. "I only wanted to tell you what will happen now. There is, first, another charge to be added, that of conspiracy to murder. I know you didn't murder Lee, but you were part of a double murder, in other words you had knowledge that it was to take place, and you did provide the ring."

Taylor read her the charge and cautioned her, and asked her if she understood and wished to say anything in reply. She said she had nothing to say except that it was the thought of losing the stables which had made her act as she had done.

Taylor told her what he had told Woodman about the remand procedure, and her appearance before the court at two-thirty.

Kennard confirmed that he would be there and would apply for bail.

"I don't have to see Stephen, do I?"

"Not until you appear at the court."

"Stay with me, Harry. I'm afraid of him. My life over the past few years has been hell. Thank God everything, the stables, the house and the horses are mine. I bought them, and I insisted that they remain in my name. I can do what I like, but what's the use now. It will break my heart, but, if Rose will buy, I will sell. I know she's interested.

"And, Inspector, one more lie I told: that story I told about hearing him going downstairs on Wednesday, that was a lie. I knew where he was going."

"Can you wait just a few more minutes, Mrs Woodman, until your statement is ready for signing. Lucy, take Mrs Woodman back to the rest room." He telephoned through to the typing office.

"Moira, put her on will you. Moira, there's another paragraph or two to add to Mrs Woodman's statement. Don't retype, just add it. I'll send Lucy in with it."

The statement had been typed and Mrs Woodman had signed it, and the WPC had taken her to the charge room for Blackwell to do the necessary. Kennard had gone, promising to be at the court in good time.

Bennett and Blackwell came in together.

"All finished, Blackwell?"

"Yes, I got your message to add the conspiracy charge, and both the Woodmans are now resting comfortably, if not willingly in the case of Woodman, down below. He was rude to the last."

"Did you nail them, Buck?"

"Mrs Woodman broke, as I thought she might. It was the bracelet, and being on her own with me and Kennard. She told all, and implicated her husband without actually saying that he killed Lee. But he had told her he would when he set her up to kill Dottie, details of every action she was to take, a step by step murder, you could say.

"He bluffed, but he had already given himself away umpteen times, and when he queried their ability to kill in the way the papers had described it, I mentioned the name Inkpen and martial arts, and he gave up, but he didn't break.

"Kennard will ask for bail for Mrs Woodman and we won't oppose it, but not for him. That we will oppose. Owning the whole shebang, as she does..."

"Everything, Inspector, house, stables and livestock?"

"Yes, Wiggy, but she's now prepared to sell if Rose Callender will buy, which reminds me that if Mrs Woodman does get bail there may have to be a surety. I'm sure that Mrs Callender would agree to be her surety but telephone her and ask her. If she agrees, ask her to be at the court this afternoon at two."

The court proceedings took just over the hour and the Woodmans were committed for trial. Kennard made a strong plea for bail for Tessa Woodman, which was supported by the police, and it was granted. It was opposed for Woodman who made the usual scene, and had to be restrained.

Tessa Woodman and Rose Callender left together. While Blackwell was settling an outstanding case of burglary, Taylor went to see the Chief Superintendent to report.

*****

Blackwell was still working in the office at four-fifteen when the phone rang. It was the Sergeant.

"Where have you been, Blackie, I've been trying to get you all afternoon?"

"The court didn't finish until nearly three-thirty. Taylor asked me to go and I wanted to go because it was a first for me. Then I went and had a coffee and a pizza at the pizza parlour, and came back here to see two villains charged, and clear my desk. Why? What's up?"

"Porritt's dead. Lesley found him this morning early. He was sitting in the kitchen with a letter in his hand. He must have heard the postman and come down and collected it. She had the sense to call the Quack. He said it was a coronary and sent for the funeral people to take the body away. Then she didn't know what to do. She phoned here but they told her we were both busy... Then she tried Rose Callender..."

"Did she say what time?"

"One-thirty."

"She was on her way to the court to pick up Mrs Woodman."

"She didn't know that. Anyway, she tried Joan, and Joan told her to try Rose again, which she did, and she was just on the point of leaving with Mrs Woodman to go to the stables, and Rose told her to go there. She's there now, but she wants to talk to you. Rose and Mrs Woodman say she can stay but she has to go back to the rectory, and she doesn't want to go on her own. Mrs C. told me privately that Lesley really wants you to comfort her."

"Thanks Wiggy. I've finished here, I hope the Inspector will let me come."

"Do I assume that the caller was Sergeant Bennett, Wiggy, was it?"

"I'm sorry, Inspector. When I stayed with the Bennetts we relaxed a bit."

"What was the trouble, come where?"

"Mr Porritt is dead, Les – Miss Porritt would like to see me, if you agree."

"Young love, Blackwell. I saw it in your eyes when you came back from seeing her instead of her father. Anything pending?"

"No, Inspector, I settled the warehouse burglary, and the two villains have been arrested and are now in cells."

"Good, off you go then. But this is important: tell the Sergeant that Bloxham wants to see all three of us in his office at ten tomorrow morning."

"I will, Inspector, and thank you."

"Use my car, I shan't be needing it."

"Thank you,"

Rose Callender opened the door at the stables to let Blackwell in.

"I'm so glad you could come. She's in there, be kind to her."

It was a small sitting room facing Coopers Lane. Lesley Porritt was sitting on a settee and Blackwell saw that she had been crying.

"Oh David," she came into his arms and he held her, stroking her hair.

"Do you want to tell me about it?"

They broke away and she handed him a letter which she had taken from the pocket of the cardigan she wore. "This is what killed him, I'm certain." The letter began, 'Dear Walter,' and, from then on, it was a death blow to all Porritt's hopes of success with his book. It was from his friend, a professor in London, who far from being friendly, had made no effort to let the old man down lightly, but had delivered a series of punches that had resulted in Porritt's knockout. 'The book, so far,' he said 'was not even accurate, the style was old-fashioned, and a best-seller on the same subject had been published only last year: it was surprising that Porritt had not heard of it.' The letter concluded, 'if the two chapters were a sample of what was to follow, give up the idea of having it published.' The correspondent had the nerve to sign it 'from your good friend.'

"You won't want to keep this?" Blackwell queried. The girl shook her head and Blackwell screwed it up and threw it into a convenient waste basket. There were still some tears in her eyes when Blackwell took her in his arms again.

"Is this the wrong time to say I love you?"

She smiled then, a weak smile, but a smile nevertheless and she answered him.

"It's the best time. I hoped you would say it because I love you too. This is only the third time we've met. It is possible isn't it?"

"For me it took only one look, it was love at first sight. The Inspector said today, when he knew I was coming to see you, that he had seen it in my eyes when I returned to the church hall after seeing you for the first time. Was it the first time for you?"

"At first I disliked you when you were so sharp, but I think it was when we met on the hill, I knew, but I didn't dare to hope."

There was a knock on the door and the two women came in.

"You don't have to say anything; I can see it in your faces. Has he asked you yet?" Tessa Woodman said.

"I haven't, but I will..." Blackwell started to say

"And I will," Lesley replied.

"I have news too," Rose Callender said, "Tessa has sold me the house, the stables, the horses, everything."

"Tessa?" Lesley said.

"I know. I know also that I shall go to prison for quite a long time. Somehow this place has lost its magic. As a matter of fact I think it was beginning to lose it a long time ago."

"I'm sorry," Lesley kissed her, "but I'm happy for you, Rose." And they kissed. "What would you say, Lesley," Rose Callender began, "if I asked you to come in with me?" Turning to Blackwell, she asked, "Are you going to continue with your police work when you are married?"

"Are you, David?"

"Yes. I've thought it over, I had doubts, but this investigation has proved that I can be part of a team. I like that, and I'd like to continue to work with Inspector Taylor and Sergeant Bennett."

"If you are willing to help me, Lesley, and David will be based in this area still, I want you to have this house..."

"Rose!"

"Yes. I thought I might have to leave the White House, and I hated the idea because I promised my husband I would never let it be sold in my lifetime."

"And you can stay here with me until the trial," Tessa said.

"I have to clear my things out of the old rectory. The rent is paid until next Wednesday but I don't want to go back there. Will you come and help me now, please David?"

"No problem, I have the car and I'm free until tomorrow morning. Which reminds me, I must phone the Sergeant."

"You can do it from the rectory. Thank goodness I don't have any furniture to move, almost everything in it is rented and belongs to the church commissioners. Are we ready?"

"Come on then."

While Lesley began looking for her father's papers in his study, and putting her clothes and other personal articles together, Blackwell phoned Bennett and told him about their appointment with Bloxham in the morning. Lesley had told him that their solicitor was Kennard, and Blackwell phoned him as well.

"Mr Kennard, this is DC Blackwell."

"Hello Blackwell, no snags I hope?"

"No Sir, this is something quite different. I'm at the old rectory. You probably don't know that Mr Porritt died this morning..."

"I did not know. How is Lesley taking it, and without being rude, how are you concerned?"

"We are engaged, Sir. I understand that you were Mr Porritt's solicitor."

"Yes, and his executor. His papers and his will are in a grey metal box he kept in a cupboard in his study. If you can let me have them I can get busy. I'm sorry I can't come at the moment; this Woodman business has put me behind. Have any arrangements been made for the funeral?"

"Hold on please, Mr Kennard. Lesley."

"What is it David?"

"I'm speaking to Mr Kennard; he is your father's executor. He's told me where his papers are. What was the name of the funeral people?"

"Francis Atkins & Company."

"Mr Kennard?"

"I heard, Blackwell. Let me have the box tonight if possible. I'll be here until seven-thirty."

"I will. Thank you, Mr Kennard."

"And give Lesley my condolences. The congratulations must wait."

Blackwell went into the study with Lesley and they found the box in the cupboard. Lesley had collected her oddments together in two suitcases and wondered what to do with her father's clothing.

"The Salvation Army will be glad to have what they consider to be useful. We can get in touch with them later. Let's get you back to the stables."

"Will you be staying, David?"

"I have to take this box to Kennard and tell him when you want the funeral."

"As soon as possible."

"I'll tell him."

Having seen her settled in the stables, they kissed and he said he would see her sometime tomorrow.

On his way back to his flat, Blackwell left the box with Kennard and told him what Lesley had said about the funeral.

*****

Friday, March 31st

Taylor, Bennett and Blackwell went together into the Chief Superintendent's office on the stroke of ten. There was a chair for each of them facing Bloxham across his desk. It was strange to sit in the presence of authority for Bennett and Blackwell, and they shifted uneasily until Bloxham spoke.

"It is a pleasure to congratulate the three of you on a job well done. Two murders solved within a matter of four days must, I think, be a record, and it was all down to good detective work, ably assisted by the uniformed branch." He smiled at Bennett.

"But that is not all. Congratulations have come from the commander of the task force and the Assistant Chief Constable. The ACC commented particularly on the brilliance of that part of the investigation into the apparent suicide of Lee which you found to have been murder.

"That is, as they say, the good news. The bad news is that DCI Brotherhood, who went into hospital for a routine operation, was found to have terminal cancer. He has little time left, and applied for permission to retire on medical grounds. His application was granted, and he retired with effect from today on full pension. He is too ill to come and say goodbye, and has requested no visits from anyone here. That is understandable. However, I propose that a letter of thanks and regret, signed by all personnel, should be sent to him."

"May I speak for the others, Chief Superintendent, when I say that we may have had our ups and downs with him sometimes, but we all respect him for the good copper he was." Taylor said.

"Thank you Inspector. Now to changes caused by his retirement. I am pleased that we are to be allowed to retain the rank of DCI but it means that the rank of DI will not be retained. Instead, we will be allowed to have a DS in CID instead of DC.

I have put forward my recommendations for these ranks. DI Taylor is recommended for Detective Chief Inspector..."

Bennett smacked Taylor on the back and Blackwell looked across and mouthed, "Well done."

"Could we reserve congratulations until I've finished, Sergeant?"

"Sorry Sir."

"For the rank of Detective Sergeant I have recommended an accelerated promotion for DC Blackwell, who, DI Taylor and I both agree, has handled himself admirably in his first two murder cases.

"You, Sergeant Bennett, were, DI Taylor reports, a source of inspiration in the help and suggestions you made throughout the investigation. There is no vacancy at present for a DI in the uniformed branch, but Inspector Horwood has told me that he will retire on 30th September. I have no doubt about my recommendation for you to succeed him."

"I shall miss my community work, Sir, but I would like to move up." Taylor looked at the others and all three stood up to attention. "I am speaking for the others, I know, when I say that we are grateful to you personally for your consideration and your thanks. I am certain that it would not have been possible to achieve what we did unless we had operated as a team, without a single word out of place from anyone."

Bloxham shook hands with each one.

"I'm sure you'll be celebrating in advance."

"Yes, and we'd be delighted if you could be there if only for a little while."

"Just let me know the date and I will come."

The three men were drinking tea in the CID room.

"When's it going to be, Buck?"

"It depends. Young Blackwell has got himself engaged but his girl is in mourning. Has the date for the funeral been settled yet?"

"It's up to Kennard..."

"Kennard?"

"Yes, isn't it a coincidence, he was Mr Porritt's solicitor and also his executor. Lesley wants it to be Wednesday and I told him, last night."

"Alright. What about Wednesday week? Joan might like to come, Wiggy, and maybe Lesley by that time."

"Joan will love it."

"And I think Lesley will, by then."

"Rose & Crown, half-seven OK."

Blackwell and Bennett agreed, and Taylor said:

"You know, we were very lucky. If that lad hadn't found the bracelet, and known where that box was, we'd have been up the creek. I might have been able to nail Woodman for Lee's murder, and by virtue of the ring, Dottie's as well. But I think he'd have shunted it on to his wife."

"And, just suppose, Inspector, that the weather hadn't changed, that it had remained cold and frosty, Lee wouldn't have got his boots wet and muddy, he wouldn't have left any footprints coming in to the barn, Wiggy and I wouldn't have bothered to look at the boxes, we would have had no reason to. It would have been tagged as a straightforward suicide, and the Woodmans would have got away with both murders."

"What about the light in the barn, the timing, and Woodman's lies?"

"Would you have bothered to investigate further the way it turned out, given the circumstances I detailed?"

"I do not like you at all, Blackwell, you frighten me. Does he you, Wiggy?" Bennett, who had been looking out of the window, turned round.

"I hate him. Don't have any more ideas like that, lad."

He turned back to the window. It overlooked the car park, and beyond, over the tops of the buildings in Kimpton, he could see on the hill part of the tower of the church and the oast and mill in Crowsett. The sun was shining brighter than it had done all week, and he said: "The sun's really come out strong at last. Things can get back to normal, and Crowsett will be able to go back to sleep again, thank God!"

"Amen to that," Taylor replied.